GHOST MORTEM

THE GHOST DETECTIVE SERIES #1

JANE HINCHEY

For my insider team, Fleur, Misty, Dana, Lilly, Lisa, and Marcia you guys are the BEST!

Whoever said that ghosts exist must be out of their mind.

Oh, wait. That was me. I said that. If you'd told me yesterday that ghosts were real I would have smiled, nodded, and called a shrink to fix your deluded little mind. Now it's my turn to question my sanity when the ghost of my best friend turns up in my apartment. Was it the tequila shots the night before causing this apparition? Or one too many bumps to the head — let's face it, clumsy is my middle name, it really wouldn't surprise me if I'd done some irreparable damage to my grey matter over the years.

Now I have to accept that the paranormal does, in fact, exist. But sadly, my ghost friend is lacking something besides his body. His memory. He doesn't know how he died but suspects foul play and he wants my help to find his killer. I can't refuse, I'm a sucker for a good mystery and the chance to bring my friend's killer to justice is too good to pass up.

Surprises abound as I discover a secret talent for sleuthing, not to mention an unexpected inheritance of a talking cat among other things. But the biggest problem of all? Captain Cowboy Hot Pants, or as he likes to be called, Detective Kade Galloway of the Firefly Bay PD. He's one smokin' cop, but my distrust of the police runs deep and despite his assurances that he's here to help can I really trust him, or is his offer of assistance designed to keep me from discovering the truth?

I guess I'll find out when death comes knocking on my door.

Join Audrey Fitzgerald in the Ghost Detective series, a paranormal cozy mystery featuring a cat, a ghost, and a murder to solve.

AUTHOR'S NOTE

Hey! Welcome to the weird and wacky world of my imagination. I hope you enjoy your time here.

If you love anything supernatural as much as I do, then you're going to enjoy the journey ahead - at least I think you will.

Ghost Mortem is the first book in my brand new Ghost Detective series, with more to come, so make sure you sign up for my newsletter to get notifications on when the next book is ready.

You can sign up for my newsletter here:
Janehinchey.com/join-my-newsletter

Okay, ready to weave some magic and solve some mysteries?

I'll see you on the other side!

xoxo

Jane

My name is Audrey Fitzgerald and this is how I died.

It wasn't a dark and stormy night. It was a clear afternoon with not a cloud in sight; the sun was shining and all was right with the world. Wait a second, no, it wasn't. Oh, I got the weather part right, but this story doesn't start all bright and bubbly, sunshine and unicorns. Oh no! This is the day I died. So no, all was not right in my world.

With such a monumental event looming I would have thought the skies would darken, thunder would boom, and basically the heavens would announce their displeasure that I'd been taken too early, too young, that it was not my time to die. But considering my tendency for clumsiness, I'm not that surprised, to be honest. It's an affliction I've had my entire life and I've got the scars to prove it! If anyone were to walk into a closed-door, trip over an invisible bump in the carpet, spill hot coffee all over herself, it would be me.

But I couldn't live my life wrapped in bubble wrap. Life was to be lived and that meant heading out into the big wide world and facing each day as the blessing it was. Mom and Dad always used to shake their heads and mutter, "It's a wonder she survived her childhood," whenever I relayed the latest disaster to befall me.

Being clumsy shouldn't define you, yet I could categorically attribute my clumsiness as the reason for my being fired from every single job I'd had. Usually, it involved spilling a hot beverage on someone. Typically the boss. On more than one occasion—because they're not monsters, they're not going to fire someone for spilling a drink. But after a trip to the ER with burns on your, er, delicate bits from the coffee I'd just spilled in your lap, the word "liability" starts to get thrown around, and rightly or wrongly, I would find myself performance managed out the door.

So my career, such as it was, was as a professional temp. Despite the fact that I'd completed a legal secretary certificate program, had a diploma in business administration and a small business management certificate, I could not hold down a job. Not for long, anyway. Because one way or another I'd screw it up. I'd dropped my fair share of expensive laptops and phones and knocked over vases on reception desks—the water splashing all over the receptionist's computer is just a given.

Don't get me wrong, I'm not bitter. Not at all. I love temping, I love the freedom and flexibility. It's the whole try before you buy scenario, and it pays well. But it means buying my own place is out of reach. No bank is going to lend me money without employment stability. I drive a rust bucket of a car. I live in a tiny apartment in a shady part of town. Until I've saved up enough to upgrade my car and the miracle of homeownership should befall me, I'm stuck where I am.

The pressure is on from my siblings too. I'm the youngest of three, and at twenty-nine the clock is ticking to settle down, get married, buy a house, have kids. Although I admit the thought of having kids is terrifying because just taking care of myself is a mountain of work already. But I figure if I could find a lovely man to be my husband, he'd make sure the kid was okay, right? Only where do you find them? The decent men? Besides my dad, there is only one other decent man I know, and he's my best friend, Ben Delaney. And there is no way Ben and I are getting hitched. Just no. We grew up next door to each other and have been besties since kindergarten. We know each other way too well to ever be romantically involved. Ever.

I suppose I'm doing my brother a disservice when it comes to decent men. He's okay, I guess. He's the eldest, is married to Amanda—who is younger than me, adding salt into the wounds of singleness—and they have two of the most beautiful children I've ever seen. Madeline, who's three, and Nathaniel, who's one. Amanda is a paralegal at Beasley, Tate, and Associates, and I briefly temped there while she was on maternity leave. Needless to say, it didn't end well and caused Amanda a certain degree of embarrassment that her sister-in-law was such a disaster.

Despite being younger than me by two years, Amanda acts way older. She's a twinset and pearl-wearing type of girl who talks as if she has a plum in her mouth. Just last week at our regular family dinner at Mom and Dad's, when the topic of conversation rolled around to my klutzy behavior like it did every week, she announced that "slower processing speed and reaction time may predispose certain individuals to errors in coordination which can lead to unintentional injuries." I'd laughed, reached for my glass, and promptly spilled red wine all over the table. She'd arched a perfectly manicured brow and said, "Case in point."

My older sister, Laura, is married to Brad, and they have one kid, baby Isabelle. Needless to say, at every family get-together my ovaries are fit to burst at all the baby cuteness surrounding me. Not to mention the tick-tock of my approaching thirtieth birthday.

But I digress. I was about to tell you how I died. Well…not died…exactly. Nearly died.

I'd started my morning by dropping my phone on my face while lying in bed. The alarm had woken me from a deep sleep and I'd snatched the phone and practically catapulted it into my forehead. I'd spent an extra ten minutes covering the angry red mark with makeup while rummaging through my wardrobe trying to find a blouse without a stain down the front. I finally settled on a white T-shirt, wearing it back to front to hide its stain. I made a mental note to ask my mom about stain removal tips—either that or buy a whole new wardrobe. Slipping my navy blazer over the top, I eyed myself critically in the mirror. No one would ever know. Provided I kept the blazer on all day.

Thankfully the matching navy skirt was dark enough to hide any marks, and sliding my feet into my heels, I rushed out the door. Stockings were pointless—nine times out of ten I'd arrive at work with a run in them. Don't ask me how, they just seemed to magically appear.

The day had gone remarkably smoothly, as far as days go. Up until three in the afternoon.

"Audrey!" Mr. Brown bellowed. I cringed, figuring my luck had run out. I'd really hoped he hadn't heard the almighty crash preceding his bellow. I'd pushed through the board room doors with my backside, carrying a heavy tray piled high with crockery ready for the meeting at four. A very important meeting with very important people. VIPs. I'd been told a dozen times to make sure the room was perfect—and to make myself scarce as soon as it was. I would not be required to take notes.

How was I to know the princess and her pony were in there getting ready for their big presentation? I didn't mean for the door to swing

back and hit the princess. FYI, she's not a real
princess; that's just what I call her. Better than
pompous ass. She struts through the office as if she's
better than everyone else and that grates on me. A
lot. And her assistant, whom I affectionately call the
pony since she's always riding him—in more ways
than one—was always on hand to see that her every
whim, every small desire, was met. She was, of
course, Mr. Brown's daughter. Untouchable.

Only I'd touched her all right. The door smacked
her in the butt so hard she catapulted into the pony
who staggered back, tripped over a cord and pulled
the whole podium, complete with laptop, onto the
floor. Of course, I lost my balance and the tray
carrying all the cups, saucers, glasses and jugs of
juice went flying, hitting the floor with a crash.
Shards of broken crockery flew through the air, and
juice splashed the floor, walls, the princess and her
pony. Pretty sure the laptop was screwed too.

"Audrey!" Mr. Brown's voice was closer now, his
footfalls heavy as he thundered down the corridor
towards the board room. I looked at the mess on the
floor, debated my chances of clearing it up before he
got here, calculated I had less than zero chance, and
figured I shouldn't even bother. I was going to get
roasted with a capital R. Especially when Mr. Brown

got an eyeful of the princess, a big wet stain spreading across the front of her silk blouse. Sucking in a deep breath, I let it fill my lungs before slowly breathing it out, waiting for the inevitable explosion. It came seconds later, the door slamming back so hard it hit the wall behind it and chipped the plaster.

I pointed to it. "That wasn't me!"

Mr. Brown's eyes bulged, his ruddy cheeks and bulbous nose became even redder, and his wide girth jiggled as rage built inside him. His hand clenched into a fist, relaxed, then clenched again and I just knew he wanted to punch me in the face. Literally. Thankfully he had more sense than to risk a potential lawsuit.

"Out!" He pointed at the door. "Get out and don't come back. You're fired!"

I skirted around him, keeping out of reach just in case he forgot himself and decided to give me a clip around the ears as a farewell present. Hurrying back to my cubicle, I quickly gathered up my belongings.

"Oh no." Joey poked his head over the divider between our cubicles and watched as I shoved my lip balm, phone, and a pad of Post-it notes into my bag.

"Yep." I nodded. "I warned you not to get attached." Slinging my bag over my shoulder, I beamed at him. "See ya, Joey. Thanks for everything. Good luck with the presentation today. I'm sorry I left such a mess for you to clean up."

"Audrey, wait." Joey hurried after me. Stopping at the elevator, I jabbed at the button, keen to be gone before Mr. Brown re-appeared. I didn't want to be responsible for him having a heart attack and I feared that was the only possible outcome if he laid eyes on me again.

"Let me talk to him," Joey pleaded. "Give him time to calm down. Maybe he'll give you a second chance."

I patted Joey's cheek. "Bless you." I smiled sweetly, knowing he meant well. "But please don't. To be fair, my assignment was almost up. Lee comes back from vacation in two days."

"Oh." Joey's face was crestfallen. "Well, maybe we could meet up for drinks after work? A proper farewell?"

"Yeah sure, that'd be cool." The elevator dinged and the doors slid open. Stepping inside, I turned. "Text me the deets."

God, I thought Joey was about to cry. His eyes welled up and his chin wobbled. The doors closed and I heard him call out, "See you, Audrey." Leaning back, I waited for the elevator to deposit me on the ground floor. It didn't have far to travel since Mr. Brown's offices were on the third floor, but experience told me I was safer to take the elevator rather than the stairs.

The elevator arrived in the foyer and I hurried across to the rotating doors, concentrating hard on not getting squashed, smiling when I successfully navigated the moving doors to step out onto the sidewalk outside. I'd left my car a couple of blocks away, where the parking was free. I headed toward it, keeping a close eye on the people around me to avoid any further collisions. One unfortunate incident a day was quite enough.

Boss. You've got a message! My phone announced. Probably Joey with details of the after-work meet-up. Digging in my bag, I pulled out my phone and squinted through the broken screen to see Joey's smiling face.

Six o'clock at the Crown and Anchor.

I started to text back when it happened. It wasn't my fault, I swear. I was jostled from behind. From. Behind. But of course, that jostling had a snowball effect and I sort of cannoned into the person in front and then shot off at a sideways angle, twisting my ankle as I stumbled over the curb—and looked up in time to see a bus bearing down on me.

2

*H*ard fingers wrapped around my arm and yanked me back. The bus whizzed past, whipping my hair back from my face, only I'd now gathered momentum and with those fingers still wrapped around my arm, I swung around and hit my rescuer fair in the nuts.

"Oooof." He dropped my arm to clutch at his crotch instead. "Son of a…" he groaned.

"I'm so sorry!" He was bent over, so all I could really see were his denim-clad legs—black denim, my favorite—and his dark hair as he dragged in a pained breath. I reached forward to offer a consoling pat on his shoulder when he suddenly straightened and our heads collided with a loud crack.

"Ow!" Pain ricocheted through my skull and I

staggered backward, raising a hand to the egg already forming on my forehead.

"Jesus Christ," my rescuer cursed. "Just stand still and don't move."

I did as I was told, watching as the dark-haired stranger straightened and I finally got a good look at him. My, oh my! Red and black checkered shirt over a black T-shirt, the dark denim I loved, boots, five o'clock shadow to die for. A red mark forming on his square jaw where we'd connected. His grey eyes— surrounded by long, thick lashes—narrowed as he studied me in turn.

"Audrey, you really do need a keeper." Ben Delaney, my bestie, stepped around the man, shaking his head at me. Launching myself at him, I wrapped my arms around his neck and squeezed him tight.

"It's good to see you!" I declared, turning my head to drop a kiss on his bristled cheek.

His chest rumbled as he laughed. "Still getting yourself into trouble I see. You're a menace." He disentangled himself from my embrace and slapped the other man on the back.

"You okay?" he asked.

Tall, Dark, and Handsome eyed me distrustfully,

but nodded. "I'll live." His voice was deep and gravelly and did funny things to my insides.

Ben grinned. "This walking disaster zone is my best friend, Audrey Fitzgerald. Audrey, meet Kade Galloway. Detective Kade Galloway."

My heart sank. He was one of them. A cop. My eyes darted between Ben and the detective. Ben gave a slight nod as if to reassure me that I could trust this one, that he was okay. Tentatively I held out a hand.

"Pleased to meet you," I offered.

He looked at my hand and with what I could only call reluctance, gave it a quick shake, then slid his hands into the front pockets of his jeans.

"Pleased to meet you too, Audrey," he smiled and I blinked in surprise. The smile was genuine and revealed a drool-worthy dimple. He was the best thing I'd seen in forever...why did he have to be a cop? Ben used to be on the force. He'd had a promising career ahead of him. Until he didn't. Until they turned their backs on him and shunned him and forced him out. Now he ran his own PI business—one I helped set up.

But I'd learned something from Ben's time on the force. Cops couldn't be trusted. They twisted things to suit themselves, and they weren't above bending the law to cover their own asses. I sighed wistfully. Such a shame.

"What are you doing out here anyway? Get off early today?" Ben asked. Then he looked me up and down, eyes narrowed, and he snorted.

"What?" I did a quick inventory, checking I hadn't spilled lunch on my T-shirt or had my skirt on backward or anything else equally mortifying.

"You got fired," he deadpanned. "Again."

I shrugged. "I was at the end of my contract anyway. Two days!" I held up two fingers in a rude gesture and he swiped my hand down, wrapping my fingers in his.

"What am I going to do with you, Fitz?" He chuckled.

"Buy me a beer?" I suggested hopefully.

"Are you sure that's a good idea?" Detective Kade Galloway drawled, one brow arching over steel grey eyes. "Seems you can barely walk in a straight line sober."

I ignored him. Linking my arm through Ben's, I urged us forward. "What are you doing here anyway? On a job?" The detective fell into step behind us and I couldn't help but be acutely aware of his presence.

"Business meeting," Ben muttered, glancing down

at me. We stopped at the light and he placed an arm protectively in front of me, as if expecting me to cross against the red light.

"Ha ha." Slapping his arm away, I folded my arms. "Oh? A runaway cat? Cheating spouse?" Those had been Ben's typical cases since opening his doors a couple of years ago when he left the force.

"Actually, this is a good one."

"A step up from a cat then."

"Indeed."

"If you're finished with your meeting, how about joining me for a drink? I've got a couple of hours to kill—you can tell me all about it."

The blaring of my alarm jerked me out of my torturous slumber the following morning. Groaning, I reached out a hand, fumbling to silence the headache-inducing screech emerging from the device I usually loved but at right this minute held in extreme contempt. Finally, my fingers landed on my phone and, peeling my eyelids open, I blearily peered at the screen, focusing around the cracks.

"You've got to be kidding me." I'd forgotten to

cancel the alarm. Punching angrily at the red cross, I eventually managed to silence it, tossing it back onto the bedside table, listening as it slid across the surface and fell off the other side and onto the floor with a thunk. I pulled the covers up to my chin, rolled over and attempted to get back to sleep. I don't know how long I lay there. Minutes? Hours? Possibly days. But eventually, it became apparent that sleep would not be returning and I may as well get up and face my day.

Throwing back the covers, I slid out of bed and stumbled into the bathroom, not bothering to check my reflection in the mirror. I didn't need confirmation. I would bet money I looked as bad as I felt. Hungover didn't begin to describe it. After the bathroom, I made my way to the kitchen. It wasn't a long commute. My apartment was small, open-plan. The foot of my bed was literally my living room, sans walls.

With a yawn, I shoved a pod into my Keurig and hit the magical button. While I waited, I pulled out a drawer and dug around inside, my fingers closing around a box of painkillers. Popping two in my mouth, I turned on the faucet, ducking my head to drink directly from the flow. Wiping my mouth with the back of my hand, I leaned back against the kitchen counter, surveying my apartment. Heels, blazer and purse on the floor by the front door. Check. Skirt and stained T-shirt in the middle of the floor, en route to the bed. Check. A random person asleep on my sofa. Check.

Wait. What?

Frowning, I tried to recall last night's events. Ben had been a champ and joined me at the pub. He'd invited the detective to join us, but he'd declined, much to my chagrin, saying he'd catch up with Ben later. Ben had a drink, maybe two, and I remember playing darts and pool with him. Then Joey had arrived and Ben had left. A couple of others from the office had turned up. There were tequila shots, and then it all gets a bit fuzzy.

So who on earth had I brought home with me? And did we...but no. I was in my PJs and he was on the sofa. Nothing had happened in that department, I was sure of it. But then, who was currently snoring on my sofa?

Creeping forward, I peeked over the back. At that exact moment, he sat up and we almost collided. I leaped back in fright, squealing as I did, promptly losing my balance and landing on my rear.

"Audrey?" Ben propped his arms on the back of the sofa and peered down at me. "You okay?"

"Ben?" I blinked at him. He blinked back.

"What are you doing here?" I asked, scrambling to my feet. The aroma of coffee filled the air so I returned to the kitchen, opened an overhead cupboard, and took down a second cup. "Coffee?" I asked.

"Please." I heard movement, looked out of the corner of my eye to see him sit up, elbows resting on his jean-clad knees as he ran his fingers through his hair.

"So," I said, preparing his coffee, "what a night." I had no recollection of Ben even returning to the pub, let alone coming home with me.

"Yeah." His voice was muffled and I jerked my head up. He was rubbing his face, vigorously, with both hands.

"You okay?" Crossing to him, I set his coffee on the table in front of the sofa. "Hungover?"

He cocked his head, looking at me. "I guess? I feel...strange."

"Strange how?" Cupping my hands around my coffee, I took a tentative sip and burned my tongue. Pursing my lips, I softly blew on the black brew.

He shrugged. "I don't know. I feel weird. How did I get here?"

My eyebrows shot into my hairline. "You don't

remember?" We were both screwed if that was the case. He was shaking his head. I plopped down beside him.

"I don't either," I admitted. "I don't remember you coming back to the Crown & Anchor. I vaguely remember leaving. Pretty sure I got a cab. Damn— that means I've gotta go back and get my car."

He chuckled. "I'll give you a lift. Later. When you're sober." He waved a hand in front of his face. "When you stop reeking like a brewery."

"Ha ha. So what do you remember?" I tried my drink again, closing my eyes as the blissful kick of caffeine hit my stomach.

Ben was silent for so long that I cracked an eye open to check on him. He was staring at the wall, a blank expression on his face. I frowned. Had he had a stroke? I was just reaching out to poke his shoulder when he swung his head to look at me, making me jump and spill my coffee in my lap.

"Shit!" I jumped up, placing the cup on the table and rushing to the bathroom. Darn, it was hot, hot, hot. I quickly stripped out of my PJ pants, the skin of my thighs bright red from the hot drink.

"You okay?" Ben called.

"I'm just going to jump in the shower," I called back. Might as well, since I was partially undressed.

And he hadn't been wrong when he said I smelled like a brewery. Anyone would think I'd marinated myself in tequila. Grabbing a strand of blonde hair, I pulled it in front of my nose, rearing back at the stench. Gross. God, I must have dragged my hair through the contents of the bar—and goodness knows what else.

Keeping the water cool, I stepped beneath the spray, wincing a little as it hit my heated flesh. After a few minutes, the sting disappeared and I cranked up the heat, steaming up the bathroom. Freshly washed and shampooed, I eventually dried myself, slipped on a robe and wrapped my hair in my turban towel. I cracked open the door and peeked out. Was Ben still here or had he gotten tired of waiting? I spotted him in the same position on the sofa. Pulling the belt of my robe tighter around my waist, I went and sat down. My coffee was almost cold, but I didn't care. I slugged it down.

"Remember anything yet?" I asked.

He shook his head. "Something's not right. Audrey, I think something's wrong." His voice had taken on an urgent tone and my heart rate spiked in response.

"What? What do you think it is? Amnesia? A brain tumor?"

He chuckled. "I'm wondering if I was drugged. If someone slipped me something. This has all the hallmarks of a roofie."

I clapped a hand over my mouth, then peeled my fingers away to whisper, "Someone roofied you? That's awful! But who? And why? Have they...?" I dropped my eyes to his jean-clad crotch and back to his face, fearful for him.

"I don't feel like anything like that happened," he said, but his dark brows were drawn together in a frown. My pickled brain scrambled through everything I knew about the date rape drug Rohypnol. It wasn't a lot. All I knew was that it was a sedative and aftereffects could include memory loss.

"We should get you to the hospital, get you tested."

"Yeah. Maybe." He nodded.

"You were going to drop me at my car anyway," I pointed out. "We could do that afterwards."

"Okay, sure." He stood, heading for my front door. "I'll wait outside for you."

I'd been about to follow him when I realized I was still in my bathrobe. Duh. I turned my back, already loosening the belt when he said, "Uh. Audrey?"

"Yeah?" I was rummaging through my dresser for jeans and a T-shirt.

"I can't open the door."

"What do you mean you can't open the door?"

"I don't know." Frowning, I looked at him over my shoulder. He was standing by the front door looking helpless. The drugs must've messed up his head.

"Okay, wait a second and I'll help you. Just turn your back while I get dressed." I kept an eye on him, waiting until he'd done as instructed and was now facing the wall. Quickly stripping out of my robe, I pulled on clean underwear, slipped on a Scooby-Doo T-shirt and worn jeans and slid my feet into my sparkly pink flip flops.

"Right, let's go." I leaned down to pick up my purse from the floor when Ben said, "Aren't you forgetting something?"

"What's that?"

"Hair?"

I lifted a hand to my head to find my hair still wrapped in my turban towel. I laughed. "Oops." I studied his face. Now that I was closer I could see he had a grey pallor. Reaching around him I opened the door and held it open for him to pass through. "You don't look so hot. Why not wait for me outside in the fresh air. I'll only be a minute."

He chuckled as he brushed past, his skin prickling mine in an icy shiver as we touched. "You forget I know you too well, Audrey Fitzgerald. You will be twenty minutes minimum."

I clasped my hands to my chest in mock outrage. "How dare you."

"Go." He waved me away. "I'm going to sit here on your stairs and wait."

3

*B*en wasn't on the stairs when I emerged thirty minutes later. Okay, so I took longer than anticipated. My blonde hair is thick, wavy and tenacious, which is why I keep it on the shorter side. That's not entirely true. It used to be long, but then I had a curling iron accident and burned off a rather substantial chunk of hair. I'd had no choice but to trail my sorry butt to my hairdresser, who must be a witch because she performed magic on it. The style she suggested—a shoulder-length bob—is edgy and chic and I love it. She even taught me how to style it with ease. Rather than battling with the straightening iron to try and create a sleek sophisticated look, every day I scrunch and blast and play to my strengths, which results in a tousled beachy look that other women pay a fortune for at the salon.

"Ben?" My apartment block was old and small. Six tiny apartments crammed into the footprint of a single house. My apartment was on the first floor, and because I was on the end I was closest to the external staircase at the end of the building. Great on nice sunny days. Crap in bad weather.

I stood at the top of the stairs. I'd been expecting Ben to be sitting here, waiting. But I had been longer than I'd anticipated; I couldn't really blame him for leaving without me. And if he'd knocked or called out I hadn't heard him over the hairdryer. Hurrying down the stairs, I stood on the footpath and looked left, then right.

"Finally." Ben drawled from behind me and I jumped in surprise. Hand to my chest I turned to face him.

"Jeez, scare a girl half to death, why don't you?" I grumbled. He still looked awful, like he had no color at all. I faced the street again. "Where's your car?"

"Yeah, that's what I was wondering." He stood next to me and ran a hand around the back of his neck.

"What? You think someone stole it?"

"Maybe? I'm really blurry on the details of last

night. Maybe I didn't drive here. But I don't remember drinking. Aside from the two beers I had with you."

"So you do remember that? What do you remember after that? When you left the Crown & Anchor? You said you had work to do. Were you meeting someone?"

"I don't know."

Someone had definitely slipped him something. That was the only explanation I could come up with. The question was, why? Was it some idiot spiking people's drinks randomly? Or something more sinister? I ran my eyes over him, looking for signs of injury, but he looked okay. Just washed out. Even the blue denim of his jeans seemed lacking color. Weird.

"Morning, Audrey." Juliette, my neighbor downstairs, appeared, dressed in her work uniform. Juliette was a teller at Wells Fargo Bank and, according to her, was going places. I figured she was, like me, saving money by living in our dumpster dive apartments. "Talking to yourself?"

"What?" I snorted. "No. I'm talking to Ben." I slung my arm out to indicate the six-foot-something man beside me.

Juliette peered at me closely for a minute before aiming her keys at the blue hatchback parked out front. The alarm beeped. "Oh. You got one of those Bluetooth headset things? Sorry, my bad. It looked like you were talking to yourself. Say hi to Ben for me." She climbed into her car and I stood watching with my mouth hanging open until she pulled out and drove away. More weirdness.

"Come on then." I shrugged Juliette's bizarre behavior off and began walking. "We'll catch the bus into town, get my car, then I'm taking you to the hospital to get checked out."

"Hospital?" He snorted. "I'm fine. I don't need to go to the hospital." He fell into step beside me. I was worried for him. Half an hour ago he'd wanted to go, now he didn't.

"Ben, you can't remember anything beyond six o'clock last night. That's not normal."

We were silent for a few minutes, walking to the bus stop around the corner.

"There's something else," he muttered.

"Oh?"

"You're not going to like it."

I stopped and faced him, hands on hips. "Now what?" The hangover headache I thought I'd conquered was starting to creep back, pulling at my temples, creating tension across my forehead.

"Let's walk. Tell me what you see?"

I huffed out a breath, but began walking again. "Maybe you've had some sort of brain aneurysm," I said, more to myself than to him.

"What do you see, Audrey?"

I looked about. "I see the road. Cars. Trees. Houses."

"No. Closer. Immediately in front of you. What do you see."

"The footpath?"

"What's on the footpath?"

"Can you just tell me because I really don't know what you want me to say!" I burst out, puzzled by what he was trying to get me to discover.

He stopped walking, so I did too. I looked to where he was looking. At our shadows. But...there was only one shadow. Mine.

"What the hell?" I yelled, blinking rapidly, then rubbing my fists into my eyes as if to clear my vision. I danced around in some sort of crazed jig, and my shadow followed, as you'd expect it to.

"You see it—or rather, don't see it?" Ben asked, voice so incredibly calm. How could he not have a shadow? My brain hurt trying to figure it out.

"Where's your shadow? What's going on?" I heard the note of hysteria in my voice and dragged in a ragged breath, my pulse skyrocketing. Ben began pacing—minus his shadow. He paused and cocked his head my way, one brow arched.

"You…you…" I gulped. He had no footsteps. He was walking, moving, yet making no sound. I swallowed, raised a shaking finger to point at him. "Are you…you can't be…"

He stepped right up to my finger, not quite touching.

"Dead? A ghost?" he supplied, still sounding outrageously calm. "I think I might be." And then he stepped forward and my finger, hand, and forearm disappeared through him, where his body should have been, an icy coldness. I snatched my arm back and staggered backward, clutching my hand to my chest. I watched as my best friend—correction, the ghost of my best friend, stared solemnly back at me.

"I can't remember what happened because last night? I died."

My eyes rolled into the back of my head and my legs gave out. As darkness rushed in all I could think was Ben couldn't be a ghost. And if he truly was, why the hell was he haunting me?

J woke with a start, heart pounding, head thumping. My cheek rested against the cold, hard, gritty ground. Prying open an eye, I discovered I was on the footpath and quickly lifted my face off the disgustingly dirty surface. Gross.

"You okay?" It was Ben, crouched in front of me. Moving to my hands and knees, I glanced around. No one was about; no one had seen me faint. No one had seen me talking to a ghost. Except for Juliette. What she said made sense now. She'd thought I'd been talking to Ben via Bluetooth. Because she couldn't see him. Because he was a ghost. A spirit.

"How long was I out?" I croaked, struggling to my feet. I felt dizzy and my legs wobbled. Ben reached out a hand to steady me, then dropped it, a rueful grin flitting across his face.

"Not long. A few seconds."

I nodded, sucking in several deep breaths. My heart rate steadied back into its normal rhythm. Brushing myself off, I picked up my bag and resumed walking. Ben fell into step beside me. "Where are we going?" he asked.

"Well, I still need to get my car," I pointed out, doing my best not to sound hysterical, "and then I'm going to your house to find out what the hell happened." I didn't know what else to do. Who do you call to say "I think my best friend is dead because his ghost is here with me now"?

"Good plan." He nodded.

I snorted, ignoring him as I stomped along the sidewalk, anger starting to blossom and take hold. Anger that Ben had died. Anger that he hadn't known he'd died. And anger at myself for not realizing I'd been talking to a dead person all morning!

"Audrey?"

"Don't even," I muttered. "I'm going through some emotions right now, Benjamin Delaney, and I just need you to be quiet while I process."

Two people waiting at the bus stop turned their heads to look my way as I approached. Right. Talking to myself, again. He mimed zipping his lips and my lips twitched in response.

The bus was packed, the nine-to-five crowd on their daily commute. After a fifteen-minute ride spent with my face pressed into the unpleasant armpit of a guy decked out in construction gear, I jumped off at Main Street and hustled to where I'd left my car. Unlocking the door, I slid in behind the wheel.

Ben stood on the passenger side, bent to look

through the window at me, and said, "Check this out!" I gave a startled yelp when he moved right through the door and seated himself in the passenger seat.

"Cool, huh?" He grinned, nodding his head, apparently immensely pleased with himself for this ghostly feat.

"I wonder why you're a ghost," I commented, turning the key in the ignition, pulling on my seatbelt, and shoving the car into reverse.

"Dunno. Unfinished business I guess?"

"So…your…uh …body? It's at your house?" I wasn't sure I wanted to see what had happened to Ben. Part of me was worried that if I reunited his spirit with his body then he might disappear for good and I hadn't come to terms with any of this yet. Coming to the end of Elm Street, I flicked on the signal to turn left onto Washington. Ben lived in a nicer part of town than me. A lovely four-bedroom house in a quiet neighborhood, right next door to the woods.

His years on the police force had paid well, and he'd been smart with his money as soon as he was old enough to know digging under the sofa cushions could pay great dividends. Plus, as an only child, his folks had helped out with a deposit to buy his own place. I wondered what would happen to it now. Did he have a will? I glanced at him out of the corner of my eye. He was staring straight ahead, a muscle ticking in his jaw.

"Ben?" I prompted.

"Yeah," he finally answered. "I don't know. I wasn't kidding when I said I don't remember anything. I truly don't."

"I wonder if you had a heart attack?" Even I was surprised that I was having such a conversation with him.

He chuckled, placing a big hand across his chest. "I'd be surprised. Had a yearly medical on the force and they never picked up any potential heart issues."

"Oh."

"Hey, no need to sound so disappointed!" he protested.

I cast a glance at him before directing my attention to the windshield. "It's just that…a heart attack seems the least gross way of dying. If you've fallen down the stairs and broken your neck and your head is on backward I'll never forgive you!" It was a valid worry. The closer we got to Ben's house, the more my anxiety grew.

"I'll go first," Ben said now, patting my knee. Only, of course, I couldn't feel his touch, just a cold blast of air that raised goosebumps on my skin. "If it's … bad, I'll come tell you and we can work out a plan."

"A plan?"

"Well, you're gonna have to call the cops and explain to them how you found me. So at some point, you're actually going to have to find me. Yeah?"

"Oh. Right." Of course. Getting into Ben's house was easy—I had a key. It was attached to my keyring, hanging out of the car's ignition. Likewise, Ben had a key to my apartment. Which was why I hadn't been surprised to find him sleeping on my sofa this morning. I touched the key and sighed. "I just wish…"

"I know." He'd always known what I was thinking, had a knack for it. It seemed even in death he hadn't lost that skill.

Pulling into the driveway, I shifted into park and killed the engine. Ben's car wasn't in the driveway, but that didn't mean it wasn't in the garage. Climbing out, I slammed the door and locked it and stared up at the house Ben called home. It was gorgeous, painted a soft grey with white trim, high-pitched roof with three dormer windows letting in light to the upstairs rooms. Along the front was a wide verandah, white posts with an American flag proudly on display. He kept the place immaculate. The curved paved path leading to the front door was swept clean of debris, the flower bed between the path and house blooming in a riot of color, the other side of the path a wide expanse of green manicured lawn.

Slowly I approached the front door. A discreet plaque to the right announced Delaney Investigations and beneath the plaque, a bell. Guess Ben now had a new case. Finding out how he died.

4

*S*tepping through the front door, Ben announced, "It's okay, you can come in. I'm not here."

"What about…" I hesitated.

"Thor? Why are you so afraid of him? He loves you." Ben laughed.

"Thor is a furry asshole who is plotting my demise," I objected.

Thor is Ben's cat, a big grey beast of a thing who looks like a teddy bear except he has homicidal tendencies. Every time I sleep over I wake to find myself being smothered by the face-hugger. He does it on purpose, I'm sure, just to freak me out.

"Anyway, he's not here. Probably found a sunny spot out back."

Glancing around to make sure his neighbor, Mrs. Hill, wasn't watching, I unlocked the door and let myself inside, quietly locking the door behind me.

"Why are you...sneaking?" Ben quizzed, head cocked to one side.

I shrugged. "The last thing we need is Ethel over here sticking her nose in." She was a lovely lady in her seventies, but Ethel was what Ben called "a little bit extra." She was a floral dress-wearing, pearl-clutching, hair-set-in-rollers-every-day busybody.

"You've let yourself into my house dozens of times. This is no different."

"Uh, yeah, it is." My voice dripped sarcasm. "You're dead, for one."

"But I'm still here, and we can work with that." The front door opened into a foyer with a staircase leading upstairs to one side, a large square archway leading to the open-plan living and kitchen areas on the right, and a passageway on the left that led to Ben's office, a bathroom, and a spare bedroom. A spare bedroom where I'd spent many a night after a boozy barbecue. I shook off the melancholy memory.

"Now what?" I asked, having no idea what we should do next.

"Search for evidence. My car is in the garage. So I

came home last night. Someone has been here. We just need to prove it."

Ben headed toward his office and I followed. "Are your ghostly senses telling you that someone has been here?" I inquired, curious about what new powers he had.

"No," he said drolly, "I can smell it. Can't you? The bleach?"

I sniffed the air, then followed my nose. He was right. I could smell bleach, and as I continued to sniff the air my nose led me to the kitchen. I was about to toss my bag on the island bench when Ben shouted, "Stop!" I froze, clutching my bag to my chest and glancing around in fear. Was whoever doused the place in bleach still here? Was I in danger?

"Don't touch anything. I don't want your fingerprints contaminating the scene." He rushed off, only to return two seconds later, gesturing for me to follow. "Come on, I can't pick the darn things up."

Following him back to the office, I asked, "Pick what up?"

"Gloves. Pull on a pair of latex gloves, and maybe pull your hair up so you don't drop strands of it all over the place."

"Why? I've been here tons of times, my prints are probably all over this place."

"You haven't been recently. I just don't want you contaminating the crime scene. The rest of the house I don't care about."

"Fine." I rummaged in my bag, found a hair tie, and pulled my hair into a ponytail. It was only just long enough and strands escaped to brush against my neck. There went all that blow drying effort.

Ben stood impatiently by his desk, pointing at the second drawer. Rolling my eyes, I crossed to the desk, shooing him away with my hands. He opened his mouth to say something, but I held up my hand to silence him. "I've got this." Stretching out the hem of my T-shirt, I gripped the drawer knob through the fabric and tugged it open.

"Smart." Ben nodded in approval.

"I'm not just here for my good looks." Inside the drawer was an open box of latex gloves. I plucked two from the box and snapped them on. "I feel like I should make an inappropriate joke at this point." I grinned.

Ben ignored me and I stuck my tongue out at his departing back.

"I saw that."

I cocked my head, wondering if ghosts had the ability to see through the back of their heads.

He laughed. "You're too predictable, Fitz."

"How dare you!" I gasped in mock outrage, following him back to the kitchen. My nose was becoming accustomed to the scent of bleach, but there was no doubt someone had used it liberally and very recently. No wonder Thor had made himself scarce. To his delicate nose the place would reek.

"It wasn't you, was it?" I asked, heading for his walk-in pantry.

"Me what?"

"On some sort of cleaning frenzy? I mean, you do keep this place like a show home. It's pristine!"

"Nothing wrong with that." He huffed, sounding put out. "But no. I don't use bleach. I use earth-friendly products."

"You so do." I was eyeballing the cleaning supplies he kept in the pantry. Alongside a bottle of Eco-Me all-purpose cleaner was a 32-ounce bottle of Aunt Fannie's Floor Cleaner. Eucalyptus. His house sure didn't smell like eucalyptus now.

"So." I stepped out of the pantry and looked around the kitchen, hands on hips. "Where did they use the bleach? And why?"

"Do I have to point out the obvious?"

"Well yeah, I guess you do, because, Mr. I-used-to-be-a-cop-and-now-I'm-a-PI, none of this comes naturally to me. Put me in front of a spreadsheet and I'll be all over it, but this?" I indicated his kitchen. "No clue. So tell me, Sherlock, what am I looking for here?"

He looked contrite. "Sorry, you're right. My bad. You're looking for blood. I suspect I was killed here and someone cleaned up the mess with bleach. We have to hope they missed a spot. It'll be small—minuscule—and easily missed."

I blanched. His blood. I mean, it was perfectly obvious, only it hadn't been for me. What did I think I was doing, standing in his kitchen with latex gloves on, playing detective? I needed to call the cops, let them deal with this. Seeing the panic on my face, he stepped up close, so close a chill emanated from him, making me shiver.

"Take a breath." His voice was firm and calm. I closed my eyes and sucked in a breath through my nose, felt my lungs expand, and held it for a few seconds before slowly releasing it through my mouth. "Good girl. You've got this. You're smart—and you're not alone. I'm right here with you."

I opened my eyes and blinked, gathering myself.

"Right. Stand back, Sherlock, you're giving me chills." I waved him away and he obediently took several steps backward. "So, where would you suggest I look, 'cause standing here, I'm seeing nothing."

"Get your phone. You've got a flashlight app, right?" I nodded. "Then get down on your hands and knees. Look along the baseboards and under the lip of the cupboards. Because of the bleach, I wouldn't expect to get anything viable off the floor, but blood has a tendency to splash around."

I'd left my bag in his office so I hustled back to retrieve my phone and then spent the next ten minutes crawling around on his kitchen floor. So far, nothing. I sat back on my heels, letting the blood rush from my head and my eyes idly drifted over to Thor's food and water bowls. Something was off with them. I cocked my head.

"What is it?" Ben asked, following my line of sight. "Ah! Good eye!" He grinned, rushing to the bowls. "They've been moved. Water goes on the left, food on the right. And look, kibble on the floor. Thor loves his food, he'd never leave kibble on the floor."

I chewed my lip and joined him. "So someone moved them—in a hurry, causing some of the kibble to spill. And look, this one's soggy. The water spilled too."

"Pick them up, look underneath," Ben urged. Carefully I picked up the water bowl and moved it to one side. Nothing but a couple more soggy kibble nuggets. But when I picked up the food bowl, I gasped. One small, tiny, drop of blood. Dried and brown. Easily missed, easy to mistake for kibble at first glance.

"Yoooo Hoooo!" A woman's shrill voice called from the rear sliding door, followed by the sound of the glass being tapped. Letting out a yelp, I dropped the food bowl, hurriedly covering the drop of blood.

"What does she want?" I hissed, trying not to move my mouth as I met the eyes of Ben's neighbor, Ethel Hill. Damn it, I thought I'd managed to sneak under the radar and avoid her detection. Should have known better.

"Don't be so hard on her." Ben rested a hand on my shoulder and I swiped his icy cold grip away. "She's a widow. She gets lonely."

Sighing, I clambered to my feet and crossed to the door, ripping off the latex gloves and stuffing them into my back pocket. I flicked the lock and slid it open but blocked entry with my body. "Mrs. Hill," I greeted her. "What can I do for you?"

"Good morning, Audrey, how wonderful and relaxed you look." She eyed me up and down, clearly finding my jeans and T-shirt lacking. "I wanted a word with Ben, please."

"He's not here." I crossed my arms to let her know I meant business when it looked like she was considering forcing her way inside. We couldn't afford to let her contaminate the crime scene.

"Where is he?" she demanded, eyes darting past me as if expecting to catch me out in a lie and find Ben sitting at the table.

I shrugged, not sure how to answer that one. The truth was, I didn't know where he was. Not his physical body, anyway.

"What are you doing in his house if he's not here?" She huffed. "That's trespassing!" Oh. My. God. Mrs. Hill cemented my opinion that she was one crazy lady. She'd seen me coming around visiting Ben ever since he'd moved in. Trespassing, my ass.

"Jesus Christ." Ben groaned, shaking his head. "Talk her down, will you?" he pleaded. "Tell her you're here to feed the cat. That'll explain what you were doing when she arrived."

"Good idea," I replied, only to have Mrs. Hill narrow her eyes at me.

"What's that?" She twisted the pearls around her neck.

"I said, I'm here to feed Thor. Ben asked me to drop in and make sure Thor had enough food and water. He's on a case, may be gone a while."

"Oh." Her hands fluttered and she clasped them together. "Well. That's good then. But he really should tell me when strange people are visiting his house. I thought you were an intruder."

"I'm hardly a strange person or an intruder, Mrs. Hill. You've seen me coming and going dozens of times. You know my car," I pointed out.

"You really should park on the street." She smoothed her palms down the front of her pink floral dress. "Ben is going to have a devil of a time getting those oil stains out. It's quite inconsiderate of you. Bringing down the tone of the entire neighborhood, that car of yours."

It was a herculean effort not to roll my eyes. I bit my tongue. In the distance, I heard a dog barking and pounced on the interruption with glee.

"Is that Percy?" I asked.

"Percival. His name is Percival." She sniffed, glancing toward her yard.

"Sure." I called him Percy to get under her skin, a little payback for her backhanded insults and thinly veiled criticisms. She thought the sun shone out of Ben's behind and that I simply didn't measure up. Not in the friend department or anything else.

"You should check on him, Mrs. H," I prodded, stepping outside and sliding the glass door closed behind me. "You know a barking dog like that could be considered a nuisance."

She gasped, hand at her throat. "My Percival a nuisance? Oh, I don't think so, although, you could be onto something. He has been getting out lately."

I placed my arm around her shoulder and guided her across the lawn and back to the gate adjoining the two backyards. She stood in the opening, her hand resting on the old wooden slats. I eyed it, betting this was Percy's escape route. It looked old and rickety, as if a strong breeze would knock it off its hinges. It had a strange burn mark on one of the planks, and as I leaned forward to get a closer look Mrs. Hill's hand covered it.

"I do hope Ben is okay," she said. "There was a bit of a fuss at his house last night. I nearly called the police."

I froze. "Oh?" I squeaked. I cast a glance back at the house. Ben had stayed inside while I'd walked Mrs. Hill back home.

"Mmmm." She nodded. "Some sort of altercation.

I heard raised voices, and you know Ben. He's not one to shout, so of course, when I heard such a ruckus I got up and peeked out the window."

"What time was this?"

"Oh, quite late. Nearly ten thirty I think."

"Did you see anything?"

"By the time I got my dressing gown on, the shouting had stopped. When I looked I could see Ben moving about in the kitchen."

"Did you see anyone else?"

Mrs. Hill looked at me. "No, I didn't. I watched for a little bit to see if I could see who Ben had been shouting at, but then I gave up and went back to bed. I thought maybe he'd been mad at Thor for something and was shouting at the cat."

If there was one thing I knew for sure, it was that Ben would never yell at his cat. He and Thor were tight. No, if Ben had been yelling at anyone, it was his killer.

5

"*S*omeone was here! Last night!" I burst back inside, frowning when I caught Ben on his hands and knees. "What are you doing?"

"Trying to move Thor's bowl," he grumbled, his tongue poking out in utter concentration as he ever so gently placed his fingers against the side of the bowl and pushed, only to have his hands disappear up to the knuckles.

"Damn it," he cursed, sitting back and resting his fists on his thighs. "Wait, what did you say?"

"I said, Mrs. Hill heard shouting—from here—last night. Around ten thirty."

"Did she see anything?"

I shook my head. "Nope. But it gives us a time frame, right? So we know you were…hurt…here. At around ten thirty. Whoever did it had to"—I coughed, clearing my throat—"dump your body. Then clean up."

"And you said you weren't good at this," he drawled, standing up.

"She said after the shouting she saw someone moving around in the kitchen. She thought it was you."

"Only it wasn't. I'd imagine the shouting stopped when I was killed. So whoever she saw was the killer."

"It has to be a man, then. Because she thought it was you."

"Is she a reliable witness though?" He was pacing now and I figured he was talking more to himself than to me. "She's an old lady."

"Not that old," I pointed out. "In her seventies, which isn't old these days."

"How clearly could she see between our houses? And it was dark. How reliable is her statement?"

"I couldn't say. It may have been dark, but your kitchen light was on. There's no way someone cleaned up with the lights off."

"Valid." He nodded. "I checked my car while you were talking to Mrs. H. No blood."

"So whoever moved you used their own vehicle."

Risky. If it had been me I'd have used Ben's vehicle and then torched it, destroying the evidence. Not that I'd ever considered murdering anyone, but you see it in the movies all the time. Dump the body, burn the car. Even better if you could make it look like the victim had been behind the wheel at the time.

"I don't think they used a vehicle at all." Ben jolted me out of my thoughts.

"Oh?"

"Mrs. H. said there was shouting, so the killer was already worried about drawing undue attention. Nosy neighbors and all that. Hell of a risk to then drag my body out the front door."

"Good point," I conceded. Mrs. H. had been on the lookout. She'd have seen if anything remotely looking like a body being stashed in a car had occurred out front of Ben's house. "But then...where are you?" A shudder wracked me. "You're not... here...are you? Hidden in the basement? And what about Thor? We thought he was outside, snoozing in the sun, but what if the killer...?" I couldn't bear the thought that someone would kill an innocent feline.

"Thor doesn't like strangers. He would have hidden. Especially if there was shouting. And the stench of the bleach has probably kept him away.

Relax, Fitz, I'm sure he's fine." He smiled widely. "Although your concern is touching."

"Shut up," I grumbled. I waved my hand around. "Can you at least go and check that you're not shoved in a wardrobe or cupboard somewhere? Please!"

"Fine." He disappeared. He either moved lightning fast now that he was a ghost, or he'd been bestowed with the power of teleportation, for as quickly as he'd disappeared, he returned.

"Nothing. My body is not in this house."

I'd walked over to the sliding back door and was looking outside, trying to catch a glimpse of grey fur, surprised how worried I was about Ben's darn cat. Ben's house was at the end of the street, Mrs. Hill one side, woods the other. Perhaps Thor had a favorite place in the woods to sleep. As I pondered the million different hiding places one cat could feasibly have, another thought crept into my head. It was easy enough, I supposed, for someone to carry Ben's body into the woods and dump it there.

"I think..." I whispered, turning to face Ben, "that maybe your body is in the woods."

Ben's brown eyes twinkled and I blinked in surprise.

"You knew!" I huffed, affronted that he'd figured it out and hadn't said a word.

He shrugged. "I think we came upon it at the same time. You were staring out the back doors towards the woods. I could see the cogs turning."

I gasped. "Is that a ghost thing? You can see…my brain?" How gross.

He rolled his eyes. "Figuratively speaking." He pointed at Thor's food bowls. "I was thinking about the blood we found. It's over here. Away from the kitchen. And the bowls have been disturbed, but whoever it was straightened them in a hurry."

"So," I continued for him, "you're saying they dragged you out the back door. And you hit the bowls as you went past. Leaving behind that one little drop of blood. Which the killer didn't see in his haste to get you out."

"She's a natural. I knew you would be." Ben stepped through the glass door and proceeded across the expanse of lawn towards the woods. I quickly opened the door and followed.

"Call for Thor," Ben told me.

"Why?"

"Because Mrs. Hill is probably watching and I want you to have a legitimate excuse for why you decided to go into the woods."

"Oh." Good thinking. "Thor!" I bellowed, cupping my hands around my mouth, "Here boy! Good boy! Come on, Thor!" We stepped over the boundary from Ben's property and into the woods, the lush lawn giving away to hard ground; manicured shrubs to tall trees, filtering the light.

A few feet in and it was as if we were in another world lost from sight. Even the sounds were different. As in, there weren't any. No birds. No rustle of little critters in the undergrowth.

"It's spooky here." I shivered, giving a shriek when I hadn't noticed Ben had stopped and I walked right through him, the icy blast chilling me to the bone. I jumped away, rubbing my hands up and down my arms. "Sorry," I muttered, but Ben wasn't paying me any attention. His focus was on the ground where two shallow troughs could be seen.

"Drag marks?" I whispered.

He nodded. "Drag marks."

In the end, it was relatively easy to find his body. We simply followed the drag marks deep into the woods and there he was, lying on his back in a small clearing, eyes closed, Thor sitting on his chest. My eyes welled with tears at the sight.

"Thor?" I croaked, and the big grey cat swiveled his head and pinned me with his orange gaze.

"About time you got here," he said in a thick British accent.

For the second time that day, my eyes rolled into the back of my head and the earth spun as it rushed up to greet me.

"*S*he's waking up. Thor, give her some space."

I blinked, then blinked again. I was lying on the ground. Ben's cat Thor sat a foot away, watching me with interest. Beyond Thor was Ben's body.

"You okay, Fitz?" Ben asked, crouching by my side. "You've had a lot of shocks today. That's the second time you've fainted. Maybe you should get checked out?"

I sat up, examining my stinging elbow.

"You've taken some skin off." Ben told me. "I tried to catch you, but…" He held up his hands and shrugged. But he was a ghost and couldn't touch anything, including me.

"I could wash that for you?" Thor offered, drawing my attention to the talking cat.

My voice trembled when I finally blurted, "You can talk."

"No," Thor corrected. "Rather, you can understand me."

"What are you saying? That I'm speaking cat?"

"Well, I'm not speaking human, that's for sure." Thor stood and arched his back, his front paws stretching out in front of him. "But I think the more pressing matter right now is my human." Thor turned his head and stared at Ben's body.

Struggling to my feet, I staggered over to Ben's prone form. Blood soaked his shirt.

"I'd say a stab wound to the abdomen." Ghost Ben bent and squinted at the tear in his shirt. "Possibly stabbed twice. I wouldn't have died straight away. More likely bled out here."

I swallowed, looking at the puddle of congealed blood beneath his body.

"Looks like," I agreed with a croak. It was a lot of blood, and now that I was closer I could smell the coppery tang in the air. Pulling my phone from my back pocket I called the police.

"My friend is dead," I said into the phone. Ben's head snapped toward me. I eyeballed him. What? We had to do this, the police had to be involved, someone had murdered him, for God's sake. After giving them Ben's address I told them I'd meet them at the edge of the woods.

"Okay." Ben sighed, acknowledging I was right. "Let's hope they send someone decent. In the meantime, don't forget what you told Mrs. Hill. That I asked you to swing by and feed Thor this morning. Remember, they will most likely check my phone records, so don't say I called or texted. Say that I asked you in person when I left the Crown and Anchor last night. Say Thor didn't come when you called him so you started looking for him and stumbled across the tracks in the dirt. And don't tell them anything about the cases I was working."

I snorted. "That's easy. I don't know anything about your cases. You mentioned when I bumped into you on the street that you had a business meeting. But that's all you said."

"Good. I don't want you to have to lie, Audrey, but…"

"I know." I half-smiled. "Best not mention I can see your ghost and talk to your cat."

"Yeah." He nodded.

Thor strolled forward, rubbing around my ankles. "To give credibility to your story, perhaps you should be holding me when the plod arrives?"

"Plod?"

"Police," he explained.

"So you're really...British?" I'd never considered cats had nationalities before.

"I'm a British Shorthair." He sniffed. "What else would I be?"

"You speak very well for a cat," I muttered, bending down to scoop him into my arms. God, he was heavy.

"I'll stay here," Ben offered. "Less chance of distracting you."

"Okay." I followed the trail back to the edge of the woods and Ben's backyard. Just as I stepped out of the tree line, two officers rounded the side of the house. I bit my lip and remained silent while I waited for Sergeant Dwight Clements and Officer Ian Mills to reach me. Dressed in black pants and gray shirts with the Firefly Bay police shield stitched above the pocket on the left-hand side, they swaggered toward me.

I couldn't believe my bad luck. These two were my least favorite members of the Firefly Bay police force. Ben's ex-colleagues and—in my opinion—utterly useless.

Ian was in his early fifties, yet had never advanced beyond officer. No surprises there. He was an incompetent moron, and the sergeant he'd been paired with, despite being younger than him, was no better.

"Audrey," Dwight boomed. "What's this nonsense about a dead body?"

"Hardly nonsense." I bristled. Thor had stiffened in my arms as soon as Dwight had spoken, his overly loud voice no doubt offensive to the cat's ears.

"It's okay," I soothed, stroking Thor's fur in reassurance. "It's Ben. He's dead."

Ian rolled his eyes. He actually rolled his eyes, as if I was some high strung female who'd overreacted to something she'd seen in the woods.

Thor must have sensed my outrage, because he sunk his claws into my shoulder. "Easy." He meowed into my ear.

"It's probably a deer," Ian said to Dwight. Dwight's eyes narrowed as he peered at me. "What happened to your arm?" he demanded.

"I fainted. Hit my elbow on the ground." It still stung and I knew it was going to sting a whole lot worse when I cleaned it. No doubt I had dirt in it.

"Fainted," he repeated.

"Yes," I snapped. "As in, lost consciousness."

"Why did you faint? Are you sick?" Ian asked.

It was my turn to roll my eyes. "I fainted because I just discovered the dead body of my best friend."

With one arm I clasped Thor to me in an awkward embrace and pointed towards the woods with the other. "In there. On the ground. Lots of blood."

Ian sighed as if what I'd just told him couldn't possibly be true.

"Don't believe me? Come on, I'll show you!" Spinning on my heel, I kept to the side of the drag marks that led directly to Ben's body.

"See?" I stood to one side so they could see for themselves. "Ben Delaney. Dead. Not a deer and not my overactive imagination."

"Put the cat down!" Ian suddenly demanded, making me jump. Thor dug his claws into my skin and launched out of my arms, equally startled by Ian's sudden command. "You're under arrest."

6

"What's this?" Detective Kade Galloway strode into the clearing, frowning at me. "Why is she cuffed?"

It was true. The morons had handcuffed my hands behind my back, arresting me for murder. I wasn't sure if I should be relieved Galloway was on the scene or worried even more incompetence was about to ensue.

"We arrested her." Dwight nodded, chest puffed out as if he was extremely proud of his actions. I bit my lip to keep from speaking. I'd already had Ian whip out his baton and threaten me with it if I said another word. I'd merely been protesting my innocence, but after the way he'd brandished the baton as if he was looking for an excuse to bring it down against my leg—hard—I'd shut up. That's how Galloway found us, ten minutes later. Me, backed up against a tree, and Ian hovering over me in a threatening manner.

"For?" Galloway asked, hands on hips. He wasn't giving us his full attention, his eyes landing on Ben's body and then surveying the rest of the small clearing where we stood.

"Well…murder," Dwight sputtered, as if it were obvious.

"And what makes you think she killed him?"

"She knew where he was. His body. She led us straight here! And she has blood on her," Ian declared. I couldn't contain the eye roll. My eyes were really getting a workout today.

"Correct me if I'm wrong…" Galloway's voice dripped sarcasm. "But didn't Miss Fitzgerald call it in? That she found her friend like this"—he waved a hand toward the body on the ground—"and immediately called us. And the blood on her appears to be her own—from that nasty-looking scrape on her arm. Does that sound like a murderer to you?"

"She could be covering her tracks!" Dwight protested. "She killed him and then called us to throw us off the scent."

"Audrey," Galloway addressed me, "did you touch the body?"

I shook my head.

"Have you touched anything here?"

I shook my head again.

"And what brought you into the woods this morning?"

"I was looking for Thor. Ben's cat."

"Why?"

"Ben asked me to drop by to feed him." It was only a small lie and I sent up a little prayer asking for forgiveness. And that they'd believe me. "I didn't kill him. Why would I? He's my best friend." My voice wobbled and my vision blurred. Please don't let me start crying now, I added to my prayer. My hands were restrained behind my back and I'd end up with snot dribbling down my face.

"Uncuff her," Galloway ordered. Sullenly Dwight grabbed my arm and jerked me forward.

"Gently!" Galloway barked. Dwight spun me and I craned my neck to look at Galloway over my shoulder. His eyes were on Dwight and I could see a spark of anger in them.

"Good," Ben said from beside me, making me jump. "Finally someone with two brain cells is here. I'm sorry you had to go through that, Fitz."

I couldn't look at him, so I turned my attention to the bark on the tree I was facing while Dwight took an unholy amount of time freeing my wrists. Eventually, it was done and I rubbed the skin where the metal had chafed.

"You could sue them for wrongful arrest," Ben said softly. "Assholes."

I glared at him as if to say, *stop talking*. For each time he spoke, I wanted to respond, and it was taking all of my faculties not to.

"You two go wait for the coroner out front. Show her the way when she arrives," Galloway ordered the two inept officers. Once they'd left the clearing he came over to me. "You okay?"

I nodded. No. I was a bit of a mess, actually.

"I'm sorry about Ben. He was a good man," Galloway continued and my eyes overflowed, tears spilling onto my cheeks. Galloway's eyes zoomed in on me. "What happened here?" he asked, raising a hand to my arm and softly stroking the skin just beneath the scrape with his thumb.

"Fainted," I choked, trying to hold myself together.

He considered me for a moment. "Go wait in the house," he said. "I'll come talk to you when I'm done here."

"You need to tell him that you think I was killed in the house," Ben interrupted. "He needs to know there's a secondary crime scene."

I cleared my throat and wiped my nose on the back of my hand. "You might want to check out Ben's kitchen," I sniffed. "When I got here, it reeked of bleach. That may not seem like a big deal to you, but Ben doesn't use bleach. In fact, I doubt he owns any. He's kind of a greenie. Was," I corrected. "I thought it was strange. And I figured that might have been why Thor wasn't inside, because of the strong smell. So I came out looking for him, but I don't know his hidey holes, but, you know, if I was a cat, the woods seem like a fun place to hang out. And then I saw the tracks…"

Galloway nodded. "I'll check it out. Officers are in there now. You can go inside—just don't touch anything, okay?"

"Sure." I began to head out when I remembered what Mrs. Hill had told me. "You might want to talk to the neighbor too. She told me she heard shouting coming from Ben's house last night."

"You talked to the neighbor?" Galloway paused, looking at me in surprise.

"Believe me, I'd have avoided it if I could. She's of the nosy variety. Was over knocking on Ben's back door as soon as I'd arrived, saying she needed to see Ben. I'm surprised she's not here now, sticking her nose in."

"Okay. Thanks, Audrey. Go ahead, I'll catch up with you soon."

I nodded and walked away. I heard Galloway talking on his phone as I left. Ben walked with me, blissfully silent. As I approached the rear of the house the glass sliding door opened and Sarah Jacobs stepped outside. She was new to the bay, having transferred after her training in the city was complete to join the Firefly Bay Police Department. There was a big spread about her in the newspaper when she'd arrived.

"Audrey Fitzgerald?" she asked, hand resting on her belt with all her police goodies attached.

"Yes."

"Detective Galloway just called, said you were coming back to the house." Her smile was friendly, and I almost sagged with relief. I'd pretty much reached my limit with Dwight and Ian. I climbed the two steps to the deck and approached, not missing her big brown eyes zooming in on my arm. "You're hurt."

"Self-inflicted." I shrugged. "I fainted when I found Ben."

She nodded in understanding. Reaching out an arm, she placed a supporting hand on my back. "Let's get that cleaned up then." I was surprised when we stepped over the threshold that an officer was already in the kitchen, dusting for prints. Galloway had said they'd be here, but for some reason I hadn't really thought they'd be doing anything. Well, anything useful. Sarah noticed me looking and paused.

"Did you touch anything in here?" she asked.

I shook my head. "I don't think so. The door." I didn't tell her about the latex gloves shoved in my back pocket.

She nodded. "We'll need to take your prints to exclude you."

"That's standard procedure," Ben whispered near my ear, making me jump. I shot him a glare and he mimed zipping his lips. He drifted off to watch the officer in the kitchen and I relaxed a fraction. It was more difficult than I realized, not talking to him.

"There's a bathroom up here." Sarah drew my attention back to her. "We can use that."

"The guest bathroom." I nodded.

"That's right. Ben was your friend."

"Best friend," I agreed.

"So you've been here many times." She smiled,

but I knew what she was doing. Pumping me for information. I was happy to play along. For now.

"Yep. Stayed over tons of times too."

"Stayed over? Were you and he...?"

I chuckled. "No, not like that. As unfathomable as it may seem, Ben and I were friends. Nothing more. We were not, nor ever have been, romantically involved. I stayed in the guest room." I nodded toward the closed door at the end of the hall. "Ben's room is upstairs. The master suite. He has his own bathroom up there and I'd use this one."

"Was Ben gay?" she asked, motioning for me to precede her into the bathroom.

I snorted. "No. Just because he has a female best friend does not make him gay."

"Sorry." She smiled again. Smiley Sarah. "Have to admit, it is unusual."

"Sure." I shrugged.

"Take a seat." Sarah pointed to the tub, and I eased myself onto the edge, watching as she grabbed a washcloth and ran it under the faucet.

"This may sting," she warned, then pressed the damp cloth to my elbow. I hissed in a breath and snapped my shoulders back.

"You should probably get this cleaned properly at

the hospital," she muttered, her face unnervingly close to mine as she peered at the scrape. "It looks like you've got a fair bit of dirt in this."

"Probably."

"Can you tell me what happened? Today?"

I went over all the events of the morning, leaving out the part about Ben appearing as a ghost and his cat now having the ability to talk. Or was it that I now had the ability to understand him? Either way, it didn't sound good for my mental health, so I decided it was entirely okay to leave those details out.

We finished up in the bathroom, and my elbow was now throbbing. Sarah admitted she may have made the whole thing worse, rather than better. Awesome. Today was turning out to be top-notch. She led me to the sofa in the living area and I sank into its plush depths. From here I could see the kitchen, dining room, and the backyard. Sarah sat opposite and pulled out her phone, typing furiously into it. I watched her for a moment, then figured she was probably writing up my statement. I turned my attention to the officer in the kitchen, who was being very thorough. Ben hovered right beside him, critically evaluating every move he made.

Sarah's phone beeped and she jumped up and disappeared, reappearing moments later carrying a mug of steaming…something. She held it out to me and I automatically accepted it.

"Thanks. What's this?" I sniffed. It smelled herbal.

"The neighbor made it. Thought you could use it, for the shock."

Mrs. Hill. Figured. She was probably out front, gathering up as much gossip fodder as possible. Thor jumped up onto the sofa next to me, startling me.

"Thor, there you are!" I'd lost track of him in the woods when they'd arrested me.

"I wouldn't drink that if I were you," he drawled in that thick British accent. It really was adorable.

"Oh?"

"She's a witch." He licked his paw, then rubbed it over his face.

"Mrs. Hill?" I asked for clarification.

"Indeed." He continued grooming.

"Yes, Mrs. Hill," Sarah answered, and I realized I'd been talking with Thor out loud. Oops.

Leaning forward, I set the mug on the coffee table. I'd take Thor's word for it. Although witch wasn't the word I'd use to describe Mrs. Hill. Mine started with a B.

The arrival of the coroner sent the place into a frenzy of activity. Sarah was called away and I sat on the sofa, watching it unfold until my eyes started to droop and eventually I dozed off, the warmth of Thor curled up against my thigh a reassuring presence.

"I'm surprised you can sleep at a time like this."

I jolted awake to find Sergeant Dwight Clements glaring down at me.

"Now what?" I grumbled.

"Clements!" Galloway's voice barked from across the room. "Have you finished canvassing the street?"

A tide of red climbed up Dwight's neck and into his face. I assumed that meant he had not.

"But, sir…" he moaned, his voice taking on a whiney pitch.

"You want to add witness harassment to the wrongful arrest report I'm writing up on you, Sergeant?" Galloway snapped, stalking towards us. He was pissed. It was evident in the way he held his shoulders, not to mention his hands clenched into fists.

"No, sir."

"Then get to it."

Dwight swiveled on his heel and stormed out of the house, the front door slamming behind him. I thought I heard Galloway mutter the word "moron" under his breath, but I couldn't be entirely sure.

Then Galloway glanced at me and did a double-take. "Jesus!" he exclaimed. "Look at your arm!"

7

The scrubbing Sarah had given the scrape on my elbow had made it ooze blood, which had slowly crept down my arm and seeped into my T-shirt and jeans. I too looked like a murder victim.

Galloway hustled me out of the house with a face cloth wrapped around my elbow and into his car, muttering all the while about being surrounded by brainless idiots and why couldn't anyone see I needed medical attention. He held the passenger door of his car open for me and made sure I was securely strapped in before sliding behind the wheel. He clamped his phone into the hands-free cradle and peeled away from the curb so fast I was flung back against the seat.

"I'm taking you to the hospital," was all he said before hitting a button on the steering wheel and then barking out orders. I'm embarrassed to say it took me a couple of minutes to realize he'd connected the phone via Bluetooth and was actually talking to the officers he'd left back at Ben's house, and not to me.

"This really isn't necessary," I told him in a lull between calls. "I'll be fine. Ben wasn't exaggerating when he said I'm accident prone."

"That cut needs to be cleaned and dressed. When I told Officer Jacobs to take care of you, I hadn't meant she should let you sit there and bleed all over the place."

"She did clean it for me," I felt compelled to tell him.

"Well, she did a crap job," he growled.

We lapsed into silence for a bit before he glanced at me and offered a small grin, the dimple in his cheek appearing. "Ben tells me you two have been friends since you were kids?"

"When did he tell you that?" I asked, a hint of defensiveness in my tone. I'd met Galloway for the first time yesterday when Ben had left him to join me at the pub.

Galloway's dimple disappeared. "We talked last

night."

"What about?"

He snorted. "You are a nosy one."

"Did Ben tell you that too?"

"Didn't have to. But I'll give you a pass just this once. Today has been an ordeal for you."

"Does that mean you're going to tell me what you talked about with him yesterday?"

He glanced at me before turning his attention back to driving. "I'm working on something and could use Ben's expertise."

"You were working a case together?" I was shocked. That Ben would work with anyone on the force surprised me. "What case?"

"Sorry. Classified."

Crossing my arms over my chest, I frowned at the detective by my side. I had no idea if I could trust this man or not—for all I knew he could have killed Ben. And here I was, climbing willingly into a car with him. Oh my God! What if I was next? What if his concern was a ploy to get me alone and kill me?

"Audrey? You okay?"

"I'm fine," I squeaked, doing my best to control my accelerated heartbeat that was thundering in my ears. "Why do you ask?"

"Because we're here?" He rested one hand on the steering wheel and twisted in his seat to face me.

I glanced around in shock. He was right. We'd pulled into the parking lot of the hospital. The car was silent. I'd been so caught up in my own panic I hadn't noticed. I hadn't noticed because I was worried I'd just made a colossal mistake—but what I did notice was that Ben hadn't joined us. Was he still at his house? Or had he...gone? Had he moved into the light before I had a chance to say goodbye? Tears welled in my eyes at the thought.

"Big day, huh?" Galloway said. I sniffed, nodding. He didn't know the half of it. Without a word he opened his door and climbed out. Fumbling with my seatbelt, I attempted to do the same, only, of course, the darn catch wouldn't release and the harder I pulled the more stuck it became.

"Here." Reaching over me, Galloway clicked the release button and the belt slid free. I hadn't even heard him open my door and gave a little squeak of surprise. I cleared my throat to mutter a quick "thanks" and slid out, smoothing my palms down the legs of my jeans.

Walking into emergency with a detective apparently gets you preferential treatment. We were ushered through to a treatment bay, totally bypassing the waiting room. I glanced at him with a raised brow. He shrugged and I couldn't help the grin that slipped out. He knew what I meant with that raised brow. Just like Ben would have known. My face fell at the thought of my dear, dead, missing friend. Where was he? I glanced around, hoping to spy him lurking somewhere nearby, that he wouldn't have abandoned me completely, but I came up empty.

Galloway stood back with arms crossed as a nurse cleaned and then dressed the wound on my elbow.

"It's just a scrape," she said reassuringly to me when she'd finished. "Nothing to worry about."

"I wasn't worried," I countered. They were making me feel like I was being a big cry baby over it. If I'd been on my own I would have taken a shower to clean it and put my own dressing on. I wasn't entirely useless.

She ignored me as if I hadn't spoken. "Change the dressing every day. I'll give you spares. Keep an eye out for signs of infection. Go see your doctor if that's the case." She handed me a half dozen big square patches from the trolley next to the gurney. "How did this happen anyway?"

"I fainted," I mumbled, not liking to admit to such a thing.

"Fainted?" She paused and stared at me intently. "Do you normally faint?" She whipped the blood pressure cuff off its stand and wrapped it around my upper arm.

"I'd just found my best friend. Dead. It was a bit of a shock."

The nurse glanced over at Galloway who was watching the proceedings with a blank face, giving nothing away.

"Oh." She finished taking my blood pressure. "All good. You do look pale. How do you feel? Wobbly? Dizzy?"

"I'm actually hungover," I admitted ruefully.

"Ohhhhh." A whisper of a smile flitted across her face. "In that case, drink plenty of water, ibuprofen for the headache I'm pretty sure you have, and make sure you eat something. And soon."

"Got it."

We were free to leave. Galloway escorted me back to his car and I wondered why he bothered himself with me. Why not send one of the deputies? I was even more surprised when he stopped by the McDonald's drive-through and ordered burgers and fries for both of us.

"Nurse's orders." He took a burger and box of fries for himself and handed the bag to me. I accepted gratefully, not knowing how to react to this man.

8

"Where have you been?" My voice came out high pitched and whiney and I cleared my throat, trying to bring it down an octave or two.

Detective Kade Galloway had dropped me at home, saying he'd arrange to have my car returned to me and that I should rest up. He'd be in touch regarding a formal statement. That had been twelve hours ago and right up until this very second, there had been no sign of Ben.

"Sorry." It was one of those apologies where you knew the issuer wasn't sorry in the slightest—the word nothing more than an automatic response to having one's ear chewed off.

"So?" I prodded. Ben lowered himself onto the sofa next to me with a sigh.

"I was supervising the scene."

"And? Did they find anything else? They discovered the blood, right?"

He nodded. "They did. They've taken swabs. They've actually been very thorough."

"You sound surprised."

"Given the first responders were Clements and Mills, yeah. But Galloway knows what he's doing and from what I saw he's working hard to make changes in the force. I don't envy him with that job."

"You two are friends?" I couldn't keep the surprise out of my voice, but Ben was already shaking his head.

"Nope. Only met recently."

"Ahhh, the case." I nodded. Galloway had mentioned he had something he wanted Ben's help with.

"He told you?" Ben's head snapped around and pinned me with a stare.

I lifted my shoulders. "Not at all. He said it was classified, but that he wanted your input."

Flopping back on the sofa, Ben tipped his head back to stare at the ceiling. "Well, it's your case now."

"What do you mean, it's my case now?" While he

couldn't possibly be any more relaxed, I was bean pole straight, my body taut with tension. After yesterday I'd already decided I was not cut out for the P.I. business. Finding dead bodies was exhausting.

"You need to find out what happened to me, Fitz." The pleading look in Ben's eyes was my undoing. I opened my mouth to respond only to be interrupted by a big grey cat.

"Where's the litter tray?" Thor demanded from his position at the foot of my bed.

"Oh, you're finally awake." My car had been returned to me the evening before, along with one very loudly complaining cat.

"Hey," Thor protested with a stretch, "I'm a cat. It's what we do. Now about this litter tray? Or I can pee in one of your shoes, your choice."

I looked at Ben in panic. I had no supplies to care for a cat. No litter box. No food. I'd put down a saucer of water upon his arrival, but he hadn't touched it.

Ben looked from me to Thor and back again, his face lit up with a big grin. "This is perfect," he said.

"Hardly!" Thor and I said in unison, then eyeballed each other.

Ben was shaking his head. "No, you don't get it.

Audrey, we need to get you back into the house—
Thor is a brilliant cover."

"Oh, right." I got it. Wait, no I didn't. "Why do I
need to get back into your house again?"

"To access my files. My death has to be related to
one of my cases."

I cleared my throat. "Yes, well, I'm sure the police
are working that angle too," I said. "They aren't
going to appreciate me sticking my nose in."

"I already told you, you're a natural at this. You've
got a bright, inquisitive mind."

"And a clumsy, disaster-prone body," I felt
compelled to point out. "Hardly the material for a
P.I."

"And need I mention her predilection for
fainting?" Thor chimed in.

"My what now?"

"Ignore him." Ben brought my attention back to
him. "He likes to use big words for a cat." Ben eyed
Thor with narrowed eyes. "She gets a pass for
fainting. She had two very big shocks yesterday. In
all the time I've known her, she's never fainted
before. It's not an issue."

Thor raised his nose in the air. "If you say so."
Jumping off the bed, he sniffed at a pair of red

sneakers. "I wasn't joking when I said I needed to pee," Thor grumbled, his tail flicking.

"Oh no, you don't!" Scooping up the grey bundle of fur, I looked at Ben beseechingly. I'd never owned a pet before. I was at a loss.

Ben laughed. "Just open the door and let him go outside. Thor, don't wander off, okay? You're not familiar with this neighborhood, and yes, before you protest, I know you have amazing feline skills, but please humor me on this. Do your business, then come straight back. We'll leave the door open."

"Very well. If you insist," Thor rumbled near my ear. Opening the door, I set him down and watched as he trotted outside and disappeared down the stairs.

"He'll be okay?" Chewing on my lip, I swiveled my head to look at Ben then back to where the cat had disappeared, worried something would happen to him. What if a dog came along and chased him? Or what if he got distracted and got hit by a car? Or someone thought he was a stray and picked him up? So many possibilities, none of them good.

"Relax, he'll be fine," Ben assured me.

"Have you always been able to understand him?" I asked.

Ben shook his head. "No. This is new to me too,

but I figure it's something to do with my ghostly situation." A chill shivered its way up my spine a second before Ben teased in my ear. "Awwww, look at you, being a caring pet parent."

"Shut up."

My phone rang and reluctantly I abandoned my position by the door to answer it.

"Audrey Fitzgerald."

"Miss Fitzgerald, my name is Athena. I'm calling from McConnell Law Firm."

"Riiiiight…" I frowned, wondering what on earth they could want.

"To schedule an appointment for you to meet with one of our lawyers, John Zampa," she continued.

"An appointment? Why?"

"I believe it is in regard to Mr. Benjamin Delaney's estate."

I lapsed into silence.

"Who is it?" Ben mouthed at me.

Putting my hand over the mouthpiece, I muttered, "Is John Zampa your lawyer?" Realization dawned and Ben's mouth formed a perfect O.

"Hello? Miss Fitzgerald? Are you there?"

Clearing my throat, I removed my hand. "Yes, sorry, I'm here."

"Oh good, I thought I'd lost you."

"I'm here," I repeated.

"As I mentioned, we'd like to set a time for you to come in and meet with Mr. Zampa."

"To go over Ben's will?"

"Yes. Would this afternoon work? Two o'clock?"

"Wow. That's fast." Considering my unemployed status, I didn't really have any excuse not to attend. But attending made Ben's death even more real. More real than I wanted it to be. More real than I could face, despite the fact that his ghost now hovered in front of me with a look of concern on his face.

"What is it?" he whispered.

"They want to talk to me about your will," I whispered back.

"Sorry?" Athena spoke into my ear and I belatedly remembered that she was still on the line.

"Two o'clock is fine. I'll see you then." I disconnected the call and eyeballed Ben. "Care to tell me why I'm meeting with your lawyer this afternoon to discuss your will?"

Ben had the grace to look sheepish. "Yeah, I've been meaning to tell you about that, but I never thought it was going to be an issue."

"What?"

Before he could respond, Thor returned, announcing he was ready for breakfast. Knowing I had nothing in the house remotely suitable for a cat to consume, I snatched up my car keys. "Right, might as well get this over with. You coming, Thor, or will you wait here?" I felt stupid asking a cat what he wanted to do, but under the circumstances, I figured it was the best thing to do.

"I'll come with you. Your driving can't be any worse than that human from yesterday." He was referring to the police officer who'd driven my car home for me—and delivered Thor. He'd sported a bleeding scratch on the back of his hand for his trouble.

The drive to Ben's house was spent in complete silence, each of us lost in our own thoughts. As soon as I'd pulled up in the driveway and opened the door, Thor had launched himself over me and disappeared down the side of his house, presumably to the cat door at the rear.

"Guess he really is hungry," I muttered, slamming the door and locking it. Slowly I approached the house. Yellow and black crime scene tape blocked the front door.

"Now what?"

"We ignore it," Ben said.

"What? No way. I'm not going to get arrested over disturbing a crime scene. You saw how happy those two morons were to arrest me yesterday," I protested, visions of being carted off to jail playing across my mind.

Ben sighed. "You have a point." While he was busy pondering what our next course of action should be, I pulled out my phone and dialed.

"Galloway," the voice on the other end barked.

"Detective Galloway, this is Audrey Fitzgerald."

There was a moment's pause, then. "Audrey. How can I help you?"

"Look, I'm at Ben's house—and yes, I know, it's a crime scene…I can see the tape. But here's the thing. I'm looking after Ben's cat. I need supplies."

"Can't you go buy what you need?" he said. A perfectly reasonable response, darn it.

"I got fired this week." Not a lie. "I'd prefer not to be spending money if I didn't have to." Again, not a lie, not entirely. But the truth was I could totally afford to go and buy Thor anything he needed. My savings account was flush. But I needed to get into the house and this seemed the best way to do it.

"Hang on a sec." I listened to the rustling on the other end of the line, then what sounded like someone typing on a keyboard. "I expedited it for you." Galloway was back on the line.

"Expedited what?"

"The crime scene has been cleared. We've already collected all the evidence we can from the property so you are cleared to return," he explained. "Just pull the tape down."

"Oh. Okay. That was quick, thank you." I disconnected the call and glanced at Ben, who was looking at me with a grin on his face.

"What?"

"Crime scenes do not usually get cleared that quickly. Normally you'd be looking at days, sometimes weeks before the property is released."

"Oh. What does that mean?"

"It means that Galloway likes you. He pulled strings."

"Or it could just mean that it was true what he said—they've actually finished processing your house and have no reason to keep me out." I did not want to think that Kade Galloway was doing me favors because doing someone a favor meant they owed you, and I did not want to owe the police department anything. Not ever. Despite Ben being seemingly on good terms with the detective, I wasn't so quick to forget his awful treatment while on the force.

"Don't get on the wrong side of him, Audrey," Ben said, reading my mind.

"I'm not," I huffed, ripping the tape from the door and screwing it into a ball in my fist. "Just because you like the guy doesn't mean I have to," I pointed out, sliding my key into the lock and turning. "After all, I met him like two days ago. Trust has to be earned."

Stepping into Ben's foyer, I looked around wide-eyed at the sight that greeted me. "Shit."

Ben brushed past me, an icy trail following. "Yeah, one thing about the cops...they don't clean up after themselves." Fingerprint dust marred multiple surfaces. Doors and drawers stood open, the contents either roughly pushed back in or left spilled out across the floor.

"I don't suppose you have any magical abilities that will clean all this up?" I asked, hands on hips as I surveyed the disaster zone.

"Not that I'm aware of." Although, bless his heart, he stood with his hands outstretched and appeared to be trying to cast some sort of spell. I giggled, my shoulders shaking with mirth.

"Hey!" Thor trotted towards us. "My food bowls are gone!"

Ben and I turned and looked toward the spot near the sliding glass doors where Thor's bowls usually sat. He was right, they were gone.

"Evidence." Ben nodded.

"It's okay, I'll get one out of the cupboard." Thor followed close by my heel as I rummaged in the kitchen for a bowl, then filled it with kibble for him. Ben groaned when I placed it on the floor.

"What?"

"It's just...that's a cereal bowl." He was frowning and looking uncomfortable.

"Do you need to....you know?" I cocked my head toward the bathroom.

"What?" He grumbled, obviously unhappy about something.

"You know. Go pee? Or poop? Or fart?"

He sighed, shaking his head. "I'm a ghost, Audrey. I can no longer do any of those things."

"Then why do you look like you're constipated?" I demanded.

"Because cats shouldn't eat out of human bowls!" he declared. Ahhh. I'd forgotten that Ben was a bit anal, not only with the cleanliness of his home but also with things like allowing pets to eat off of human crockery.

As much as it would be fun to tease him, I figured now wasn't the time. He had just recently died after all. "We're going to have to, just this once," I said. "Thor needs to eat and his bowls are evidence. Fingerprints?"

"Yeah. We know the bowls were moved. Could be blood too."

Distracting Ben from his discomfort over watching his cat eat out of a cereal bowl I asked, "So where are these files?"

"On the computer—in the office."

Dusting my hands on my jeans, I squared my shoulders. "Come on then. Let's go see what you were working on that ended up getting you killed."

9

*P*hilip Drake was the General Manager of the Firefly Bay Hotel, a five-star establishment towering over the bay along the esplanade. The hotel specialized in fine dining, afternoon teas, and a cooking school, alongside luxury accommodation. Philip had hired Ben to run a background check on his daughter's new boyfriend.

"Seriously?" I said, more to myself than to Ben, who was hovering behind me and reading over my shoulder. "He wanted you to dig up the dirt on his daughter's boyfriend? What's up with that?"

"He's an overprotective dad. Sophie's mom died when she was a toddler and it's been just the two of them ever since."

"But a background check?" I scoffed. "Overkill, don't you think?"

I clicked through the files on Ben's computer. "Errr." I paused and leaned closer, squinting at the screen. "Gone a bit out of the boundaries of the brief, don't ya think, Delaney?" On the screen was a diagram linking Philip and his daughter, Sophie, Sophie's boyfriend, Logan Crane, and two of Philip's employees, Brett Baxter and Steven Armstrong. I tapped on Brett and Steven's names. "Why are they here?"

When Ben didn't answer I swiveled in my chair only to find him running a hand over his chin in apparent thought. "You know..." He paused, drifting off as his thought processes whirled.

After a solid sixty seconds of silence, I finally prompted, "What?"

"What?" He shook his head, snapping out of his stupor.

"The Drake case?" I prompted. "Why are these two individuals in your file?"

"I don't know." He shrugged and I knew today was going to be a level five caffeine consumption day.

"As in, you don't remember?" I sighed, the heavy weight of the truth settling over me like a wet blanket. It looked like Ben didn't recall the details of his cases. How handy.

He rested a hand on my shoulder, giving me immediate frostbite. "Sorry." And I knew he meant it. Hell, it must be frustrating for him, not remembering what had happened, nor what he'd been working on. Not to mention being dead. I imagined that would suck big time too.

Shrugging his icy hand away, I grinned. "Never mind. Looks like you've already done some work here." I opened up another file and read it aloud. "You've thoroughly researched Logan, his financial and credit history, social background, criminal record. It looks to me as if the job is done."

"But it's not closed." Ben indicated the green tab meaning he hadn't closed off the file in his system. "I hadn't finished."

"Or maybe you hadn't delivered the results to Drake yet?"

"Which is odd. Look at the date."

I did. The entry was from five days ago. Ben wouldn't have kept his client waiting any longer than necessary, so why hadn't he delivered the final report and closed out the case? Not to mention get paid.

"Philip Drake was right to be concerned—look

what you turned up. Logan Crane is a drug user, possible dealer and has priors for car theft and B&E...what's B&E?"

"Breaking and entering."

"Right. So Logan Crane is a low life. Why are you sitting on this?"

"Must be something to do with these two." Ben pointed at the two employees on the screen.

"You don't have much on them. Steven Armstrong is thirty-five and Front of House Manager. Hardly a crime," I drawled, before continuing to read, "And Brett Baxter, twenty-seven, Event Planner." I glanced at Ben again, hoping something—anything — would jog his memory. Nothing. I sighed, closed out of the Drake file and opened the next one in Ben's database.

"Tonya Armstrong. Hired you for spousal surveillance."

"Meaning she thought her husband was cheating."

"And was he?"

Ben began pacing. "Dunno. Can't remember. What does the file say?"

Frowning, I watched him, noticed the tense line of his shoulders, the clenched jaw. This was as frustrating for him as it was for me. If only he could do something useful while I went through the files—like make me coffee.

"Ooohhhh." Turning my attention back to the monitor, I leaned forward, eyes darting from side to side as I scanned Ben's notes. "He was! You had surveillance of it—but get this—she wanted further evidence. Why? Let's see what you gave her." I clicked on the attachments to the file and a dozen images opened up on the screen.

"Wait." I leaned closer, my nose almost touching the monitor. "Isn't that the guy from the Drake case?"

That got Ben's attention. He rushed forward so fast he materialized inside the table. I shot back in surprise, my backward momentum too fast. The wheels of the office chair snagged on the rug and before I knew it I was flat on my back, staring up at the ceiling.

"Shit!" Ben cursed, stepping out of the desk. "Are you okay?"

Rolling to my side, I scrambled to my feet and righted the chair. "Yep, I'm fine. Just wasn't expecting you to appear in the desk, that's all." Settling myself back in the chair, I turned my attention back to the contents on the screen. "This"—I pointed— "must be Tonya's husband, yes?"

"I'd assume so if I've recorded surveillance footage of him."

"Tonya Armstrong...married to Steven Armstrong. As in Steven Armstrong the front of house manager from the hotel?" I scoured the details on the screen. "Bingo!" I shouted, punching the air. "There's your connection! That's why you haven't closed off the Drake case—because it's connected with your cheating bastard of a husband case."

"That wouldn't be why I hadn't closed off the case. It's a connection, yes, but the fact that one of Drake's employees is having an affair isn't relevant."

"Not relevant? Surely Drake would want to know that the morals of one of his employees were ... questionable?" I argued.

"But that's not what he hired me for. He hired me for a background check on his daughter's boyfriend. My case with him has nothing to do with the hotel."

"So you're saying you wouldn't tell him what you'd discovered about Armstrong?" Ben shook his head. Shoulders slumping, I eyed the images on the screen once more. They were of Steven Armstrong kissing a blonde woman. "Do you know who the woman is?"

"I had to get the shots with his face in view, to

prove it's him, which meant her back was to the camera."

"So that's a no."

"Not necessarily. Check the notes. And there may be more photos on my camera that we can go through. I would have taken hundreds to get the money shot. I only deliver the ones that provide the undeniable proof my client is seeking."

I scanned the notes, but there was no mention of who the woman was. "It says here that Tonya wanted further proof…"

Ben shrugged. "Some clients don't want to believe the truth, even when presented with the evidence."

"But what does she mean, further proof?"

"I can't remember the details, but usually when it's a case like this, they want a video recording of their spouse caught in the act."

I gasped. "She wanted you to record them actually having sex?"

He shrugged again. "Possibly. But look at the flag there." He pointed to the bottom right of the screen where an orange tab indicated the case was ready to be closed.

"You were closing the case." No point in actually asking Ben that. The answer was, he couldn't remember. I'd been hoping going through his files would jog his memory, but so far a big fat zero.

"I don't do sex tapes," he said, drifting around the room.

"Fair enough. So you'd flagged the Armstrong case to be closed. You'd already met with your client and provided her with the evidence you'd gathered. I see she paid you a retainer, but you haven't invoiced for the remainder of your fee." Picking up a pencil, I scribbled a note to remind myself to close out the file and send the invoice.

"Third and final case." I clicked open the one remaining green tab and blinked in disbelief. "Okay, this is just weird. Your third case was Brett Baxter. The same Brett Baxter, I assume, who is the event planner at the hotel. This is too much of a coincidence, Ben. All of your cases are connected. And the common thread is Philip Drake."

"I'd say the common thread is the Firefly Bay Hotel," he argued.

"But the hotel didn't hire you—not for any of these investigations. Drake hired you personally. Tonya Armstrong hired you personally. As did Brett. What did he hire you for anyway?" Turning my attention back to the screen, I snorted. "A witch hunt? As in, he literally wanted you to prove witches are real? What the…? That's just ludicrous!" As incredible as I found it, something niggled at the back of my brain, "But you took the case… Why would you take a case like this? Some zealot who believes in magic and witchcraft? That's not like you."

"You're right. It isn't. Ordinarily that would be a hard pass. So the question is, why did I take the case?"

"Because it overlaps with the other two?"

He was shaking his head. "Check the dates I opened the other cases. At the time, I wouldn't have known about the overlap. Maybe the overlap is pure coincidence."

"You don't believe in coincidence." It was true. He didn't. It had been a long-term argument between us, and for once I agreed with Ben. It was too much of a coincidence for his three cases to be related—especially now that he was dead. Something in one of these files had driven someone to kill him.

"You don't have much on Brett. You couldn't have started his investigation yet."

"Which is odd." He peered over my shoulder again, his closeness bringing with it arctic conditions. Shivering, I pushed him away, only to have my hand disappear wrist deep inside him. With a yelp, I snatched my hand away and clambered to my feet. Ben looked contrite. "Sorry," he said.

"Why are you apologizing? I'm the one who just shoved my hand inside you!" I studied him, head cocked to one side. "Can you feel it, when that happens?" What I really wanted to ask was if it hurt when someone passed through him.

He studied me for a second before a slow grin spread over his face. "It doesn't hurt, Fitz. I can't feel it, I can't feel anything."

"When I touch you, I feel cold. Icy cold."

He nodded. "Ahhh, that explains why you're constantly shivering."

10

"He's what now?" I couldn't believe what I was hearing. I glanced at Ben out of the corner of my eye, seated next to me in front of John Zampa's giant mahogany desk, the plush tub chair curling around me in an oddly comforting embrace.

"Left you his entire estate," the lawyer repeated. "With some stipulations," he added.

I sucked in a deep breath, calming myself. This was unexpected. Yes, I fully expected to take custody of Ben's cat, but that was the extent of my involvement in his estate. How wrong was I?

"Which are?" It seemed only logical I should ask. Ben patted my knee, sending an icy chill down my leg and making me jerk. The lawyer looked at me, probably thought I was about to have some sort of seizure with the sporadic jerking I kept doing because Ben kept patting my leg to calm me down.

"You are the new owner of his business, Delaney Investigations. And—once the paperwork is complete—you will have power of attorney for his father, William Delaney."

Tears sprang to my eyes, blurring my vision. I'd forgotten about Ben's dad in all of this. Ben was an only child to Beryl and William Delaney. His mom died of cancer ten years ago, and his dad had been stricken down with Alzheimer's and had spent the last three years in a nursing home.

The lawyer continued. "McConnell's, as executors of the will, will provide you access to a trust fund Mr. Delaney had set up to cover his father's expenses. All remaining assets—the house, vehicle, bank accounts—will be transferred to you. I believe you already have possession of Mr. Delaney's cat?"

"Yes," I croaked, cheeks wet with tears and snot starting to dribble out of my nose. A box of tissues was nudged toward me and I grabbed a handful, pressing them to my face. I had never considered Ben would leave me everything. It was difficult to get my head around.

After I'd signed a ton of paperwork, I was free to

go. I stood, shook the lawyer's hand, slung my purse over my shoulder, and promptly knocked the box of tissues off his desk.

"Oops. Sorry." I quickly snatched them up from the floor and placed them carefully back on the desk.

"Not a problem at all, Miss Fitzgerald." Despite my telling him to call me Audrey, he'd persisted with calling me Miss Fitzgerald throughout the entire proceedings.

"You okay?" Ben asked as we left the offices of McConnell Law Firm and headed to my car parked out front.

"I think I'm in shock," I whispered, aware that to onlookers it appeared as if I were talking to myself. Sliding behind the wheel, I clasped it with both hands and sat for a moment, gathering my thoughts.

"Why didn't you tell me?" I finally asked, starting the engine and pulling out into the flow of traffic.

"What? That I had a will?"

"No, that you left everything to me in that will!"

"It's okay, I'm sure the cops don't think you're a suspect, that you knocked me off for the inheritance."

I blanched. "I hadn't even considered that!" But now that he mentioned it, it dawned on me that in the cops' eyes, I had motive. "Ben." I glanced at him before turning my attention to the road. "I don't even have a will. It was a huge shock that you made me your only beneficiary."

"You really should have a will, Audrey. If something were to happen to you, the state would take a huge chunk of your assets because you died without one."

"You'd need to have assets for that to be an issue," I pointed out.

"Well"—he sounded almost cheerful about this —"now you do!"

Right. Now I had a four-bedroom house in a beautiful neighborhood, a Nissan Rogue, a cat, and apparently, a P.I. business. Oh, and I was responsible for any decisions concerning his dad. Not that that was an issue. I'd happily take on board Mr. Delaney's well-being. Before he'd become ill he was an absolute sweetheart of a man. How would I tell him his son had died? No parent should have to bury their own children. It was heartbreaking.

"About your dad…"

"Don't tell him," Ben said. "He doesn't remember me, hasn't known who I am for over a year now. No need to upset him over something like this."

"Something like this?" I protested. "Ben, he's your dad. He has to know."

"Does he though? Audrey, he lives in a world where he doesn't have a wife or a son—he thinks he's sixteen years old! Look, it's just going to upset you more than it will him. The lawyers will notify the nursing home on the changes, and they'll provide the new power of attorney documents. That's all that needs to happen."

I wasn't convinced that was the right course of action, but Ben had a point. I could afford to wait, at least for a little while.

"I'm going to have to arrange your funeral, aren't I?" It wasn't that it would be a hardship. I'm a born organizer. It was just that it was another tangible truth. Ben was dead.

"Afraid so," he grinned, unrepentant.

I snorted, turned the car onto the Esplanade, my eyes set on the Firefly Bay Hotel visible above the treeline.

"Where are you going?" Ben asked, a hint of suspicion in his voice.

I grinned. "I'm going to see what—or who—I can turn up at the hotel."

"Audrey," Ben warned.

"Don't 'Audrey' me," I grumbled. "I am now, officially, the owner of Delaney Investigations, and this is my first case. That requires me revisiting your open cases. You said so yourself."

"Yes, well…" He cleared his throat. "When I wrote that will I wasn't expecting to be dying anytime soon."

"Well, you did. Sucks to be you," I teased, tossing him a wink. "I wouldn't have to be doing any of this if you could only remember what happened. Or something useful, like the details of your open cases. I don't understand why you don't remember that." I'd descended from teasing to grumbling, beyond frustrated that Ben couldn't remember what he was working on. "Oh!" Another thought hit me. "You were working on something with Detective Galloway. But there was no record of it on your computer. What does that mean?"

"Off the books," he said darkly, brows drawn together in a frown.

"You were working—with a detective of all things—off the books?" My voice had gone up an octave in outrage. "Benjamin Delaney, how could you?"

"What?" he protested. "I've worked off the books before."

"Not that. I meant working with the cops. After the way they treated you?"

He sighed. "Audrey, you have to let that go. I have. I've moved on, no point dwelling on it."

"Ben, they squeezed you off the force—a job you loved. They lied. They made you look like a bad cop when we all know you weren't. It's appalling."

"I know, I know, but it's done."

"Corruption on the force is never done." I was just getting started, my indignation rising. "Look how Clements and Mills treated me, arresting me on the spot. Intimidation." I shook my head, my hair flipping around and whipping me in the eye. "Ow." Taking one hand off the wheel, I rubbed at my stinging eyeball, tucking my hair behind my ear to clear my vision.

"Audrey!" Ben yelled. A car horn sounded and I looked up in time to see a four-wheel-drive bearing down on us.

"Shit!" With a yank of the wheel, I got myself back onto the correct side of the road and cast a quick glance at Ben. "You okay?"

"Well, it's not like I can die again," he muttered. "But I'd prefer it if you didn't join me. Just...both hands on the wheel, eh, Fitz? Please."

"Pft, it was fine." But I gave in and wrapped my fingers around the steering wheel, tight, only because Ben looked like he might just soil himself and I wasn't sure what the end result would be. Ghostly slime? Who knew? But I wasn't prepared to risk it, just in case. Although...I now had access to Ben's car. His lovely, newer than my hunk 'o junk, Nissan Rogue, with leather seats, automatic everything, a sexy gun metal grey with not a scratch, dent, or rust patch to be seen. A car he had never let me drive.

"What are you thinking about?" Ben cut into my thoughts. "I don't like that grin. It's evil."

I clapped a hand to my chest in mock outrage, remembered I'd promised to keep both hands on the wheel, so quickly slapped it back on the wheel, and gasped, "Me? Evil? How dare you. If you must know, I was thinking about your car. It's mine now." My smile was full-blown as his eyes widened into perfectly round orbs.

"Ooops. We're here!" I'd almost overshot the hotel. Slamming my foot hard on the brakes, I yanked on the steering wheel. The back end screeched in protest as it slid across the asphalt, and I glided into the parking space with practiced precision.

Ben was shaking his head and keeping a ghostly grip on the armrest. "I will never get used to that."

"Oh come on, you love it." I grinned. "Also, I've had another brilliant idea."

"Another?" he teased, as if I hadn't managed even one brilliant idea yet.

"Lucky for you, you're incorporeal so I can't punch you. Smartass. But yes, I know how we can communicate without me looking like I'm insane."

"Do tell."

"My phone. I'll pretend to be on a call. Only I'll be talking to you. Brilliant, right?"

He smiled, teeth shining white—actually they were a little too white, and I wondered if the afterlife added something a little ghostly extra. "Actually that's not a bad idea, Fitz."

"I know, right?" Pleased with myself, I unbuckled and half climbed, half fell out of the car. Straightening up, I locked it, grabbed my phone out of my bag, waggled it at Ben who was watching with one brow arched, then threw my bag over my shoulder, only to have it hit the window of my car and ricochet back on me, making me lose my balance. I ignored Ben's snort and tried again, only with less enthusiasm this time. With a happy grin and sideways glance, I crossed the street and made my way inside the Firefly Bay Hotel.

As we crossed the foyer to the reception desk,

Ben nudged me with an icy blast of his elbow, "Ahhh, Fitz?"

"Mmmmm?" I was focused on my quest. The redhead behind the counter. She was young—she looked about twelve!—but her makeup may well have been applied with a trowel, it was so thick. She'd look so much prettier if she toned it down a notch or a hundred.

"Your phone? I can't make it ring, you know. If you want to be pretending you're talking to me, you may want to at least hold it up to your ear," he prompted. Of course, he was right. As usual. With a huff, I lifted the phone to my ear, paused in my stride as if I'd just answered it—since Miss Twelve Year Old With More Makeup Than A Drag Queen had heard me approach and was waiting with a plastic smile.

"Happy now?" I inquired.

"Ecstatic." He grinned. And looking at his smiling face, in that moment he looked relaxed and happy and alive. Only he wasn't, and my answering smile slipped, and my eyes became a little glassy. I missed him. I missed him being alive.

He saw the change. "Fitz?" he prompted, concerned.

I sniffed. "It's okay," I reassured him, "I'm just having a moment."

The look of discomfort wasn't hard to miss. The typical reaction of a man when a woman says she's having a moment. As in...emotions. Gah.

Straightening my shoulders, I sniffed—an incredibly unladylike sniff—and continued to the reception desk.

"Good afternoon, ma'am," Miss Twelve Year Old With More Makeup Than A Drag Queen greeted me. "How may I help you today?"

My eyes landed on the name badge pinned to her lapel. Putting my hand over my phone so the fictitious person on the other end couldn't hear, I said, "Hey, Barbie." I mean...Barbie? Come on. "I was hoping to have a word with the manager, Phillip Drake."

"Do you have an appointment?" She was typing into the computer, eyes on the monitor. I assumed she'd pulled up his appointment calendar or whatever it was they used to manage such things.

"I do not."

"Oh!" She glanced back at me. "Mr. Drake doesn't usually see people without an appointment. He's very busy."

"I'm sure he is," I shot back. "Perhaps if you tell

him Audrey Fitzgerald from Delaney Investigations is here, I'm sure he'll make time for me."

"Nice." Ben nodded his head in approval and I automatically replied, "Right?"

"The phone," he whispered, reminding me to use it. Clearing my throat, I removed the hand covering the receiver and repeated myself, "Right?" then mouthed at Barbie, "Sorry—important call." She nodded in understanding, then picked up the landline and hit a button.

"I guess I'm going to need some business cards," I said into the phone, watching while Barbie spoke with someone on the other end of the line. I hoped it was Phillip Drake.

"I think you're really starting to get on board with this," Ben said. "I may have created a monster."

"You said I was a natural!" I protested.

He laughed. "You are. I was joking. If you get in to see Drake, you're going to have to hang up the phone. I'll let you know if there's anything you need to ask that you missed, but other than that I'll stay out of your way and do my best not to distract you."

"Right." I nodded, a wave of butterflies settling in my stomach. I was about to meet with a man who could potentially be a murderer.

"You're starting to freak out." Ben sighed. "I knew

you'd do this."

"I'm not," I protested. I was.

"The best way to approach this is to go with the truth. You'll only trip yourself up with lies."

"The truth?" I was aghast. I couldn't tell Drake that Ben was a ghost.

Ben heaved the biggest sigh known to man, complete with eye roll. "Tell him what happened to me. The dying part only. Gloss over the murder part. Explain that you inherited the business and that you want to get things squared away and are revisiting the open cases. Ask him to tell you where the investigation is at. Don't overthink it. You've got this." He slapped me on the back and an ice-cold blast shot right through me. "Sorry." He cringed, remembering what happened when he touched me a second too late.

"Miss Fitzgerald is it?" I spun to find a man dressed impeccably in a grey pinstripe suit, complete with waistcoat, approaching. He wore a smile that didn't reach his eyes. "I'm Phillip Drake. I believe you wanted to see me?"

"Here we go," Ben whispered.

Sliding my phone into my bag, I plastered my own fake smile on my face and held out my hand. "Audrey Fitzgerald, Delaney Investigations."

11

I followed Phillip Drake to his office. It was a very nice office. Not as nice as the lawyer, Mr. Zampa's, but close. Very opulent. Sinking into the plush chair opposite his very—very—wide desk, I watched and waited while he fiddled with pens and papers, moving them until they aligned perfectly. Eventually he was satisfied. He steepled his fingers beneath his chin and met my eyes.

"I didn't know Ben had a partner," he said.

"He didn't."

Phillip's head jerked a little, the slightest of movements, betraying his surprise. "But you just said you were from Delaney Investigations." His face darkened. "Are you here under false pretenses?

Because let me assure you, Miss Fitzgerald, I will not tolerate it." He was already reaching for the phone on his desk. To call security and toss me out? This had gone downhill real fast and we hadn't even gotten beyond introductions.

"Please." I held up a hand. "Let me explain."

"Please do." He paused, hand on the phone, the threat implied that if he didn't like what I had to say he'd be having my ass hauled out of here.

Drawing in a deep breath, I spoke in my most professional voice. "I'm sorry to inform you that Ben...has died." A lump the size of a golf ball lodged in my throat. This was harder than I'd anticipated. The look of shock on Phillip's face was almost my undoing. I cleared my throat. "I've taken over Ben's caseload and am visiting his clients personally to inform them of the situation and assure you that it is business as usual."

There. I got it out without bawling like a baby. Phillip slumped back in his chair, shaking his head. "I don't know what to say," he muttered, clearly shocked at the news. "What happened?"

"I can't say much, as it's an ongoing investigation, but I can tell you that Ben was murdered." I remembered a second too late that Ben had told me not to mention that little detail.

He blinked, his pale grey eyes devoid of emotion.

"He's in shock," Ben whispered in my ear. I jerked in surprise. He'd promised he'd stay out of my line of vision and keep his trap shut. Now I was twitching like a rabid squirrel, and that was not the impression I wanted to give my new client. Look at me, all professional and everything. But Ben was right, Phillip had that dazed look about him.

"I'm sorry. I know that's a lot to take on board." I nodded sympathetically. "My time is limited and I'm sure you're a very busy man, but I was hoping we could go over the details of the case Ben was working on for you."

Phillip cleared his throat and straightened his tie, visibly pulling himself together. "He'd actually finished."

"Oh? His records don't indicate that. And your final invoice has not been issued or paid," I replied. "I know Ben was conducting a background check on your daughter Sophie's boyfriend?" I prompted.

"Ssh," Ben murmured from behind me. "Let him tell you, remember?"

"Oh right," I muttered.

"What?" Phillip frowned.

"What?" I frowned back.

"I thought you said something?" he said.

I shook my head. "Nope. Go ahead." I nodded, had my phone ready to type in notes...if only I could see my screen clearly through the cracks. I wondered where Ben's phone was. I could use that. I supposed the police had it in evidence. I wondered if I asked Detective Galloway about it I could get it back. Once they'd downloaded all the data from it, surely they didn't need the actual phone?

"Audrey, pay attention!" Ben snapped. I jumped again and realized Phillip was talking. I tuned in mid-sentence. "...it's been Soph and I for so long, and she's always been such a good girl, but I think she's fallen in with the wrong crowd, you know?" He continued on without waiting for an answer. "She's been sneaking out, telling lies, stealing money. All since she's been seeing this new boy, Logan Crane. But you know teenagers, always so dramatic. Every time I asked her about him she'd storm off, refusing to speak to me. So I hired Ben to check him out. Ben told me last week that Logan has a criminal record—theft. And he's a drug user. Not the type of person I want my daughter associating with."

"And Ben provided evidence of this?"

"Ummm." Phillip hesitated and I glanced up from the phone where I'd been jotting down what he'd told me. So far it had been identical to what had been in his file.

"No?" Curious. I didn't dare look at Ben for confirmation, especially since he was hovering somewhere behind me and I'd look like a tool for suddenly spinning around to eyeball the wall.

"He may have? I just can't recall..."

My eyebrows shot into my hairline. Phillip Drake struck me as a very organized, very meticulous man. Possibly OCD by the way he kept his desk. If Ben had provided the evidence that Logan was a criminal and a druggie, Phillip would be able to lay his hands on it immediately. Which led me to believe Ben hadn't provided that evidence. Was it because he didn't have it? But why report to Phillip that he did?

"Was this a verbal report?" I asked.

Phillip snapped his fingers and pointed at me. "Yes! That's it! I knew he'd told me, but I couldn't remember if it was in an email or phone call. Now I remember. A phone call."

I nodded my head, made a note to check Ben's phone records. "Do you remember what day that was?" I asked.

"Errrr. Tuesday? Maybe. I can't really remember."

"Would it be on your phone? The last call you took from Ben?"

Phillip's head whipped around to the mobile phone positioned neatly at the edge of his desk calendar. "Why, yes, I guess it would be." He made a move to pick up the mobile, then stopped, hand hovering inches above it. "Actually, I think he called me on my landline." He pointed to the handset to his right. The one his hand had been resting on when he'd threatened to call security. "Is it important? Knowing what day he called?"

"No, no," I smiled politely. "It helps me with the timeline of where Ben was up to with things, that's all."

"Are you a relative of Ben's?" he asked.

I shook my head. "No."

"Oh. I thought you must be related, although you don't look anything alike, now that I think about it."

I frowned, puzzled. "Why would you think I was related to Ben?"

"Well, because you're here, taking over his case. I thought perhaps you were family."

"He's trying to distract you and it's working," Ben whispered in my ear, sending yet another ghostly chill down my spine.

"Not family," I assured him. "Now if we could get back to your case if you don't mind..."

"Actually I'm going to have to cut this short."

Phillip stood, and I blinked in surprise. "I've just remembered a prior appointment." He came around the desk and held out a hand. Slowly rising to my feet, I shook it and let him usher me toward the door.

"Look, I'm very sorry to hear about Ben. That is terrible news, but considering the circumstances, I think it best we sever this relationship." His voice had taken on a professional polish I recognized. I'd used it myself dozens of times. My internal bullshit alarm went off.

"Ben had verbally confirmed what I suspected about Logan. I have all I need. But please, do send me the invoice, I will pay in full, of course."

"You don't want me to send over any evidence?" I asked.

He shook his head. "Please don't trouble yourself. That won't be necessary."

"Well...okay. Thanks for taking the time to meet with me today, Mr. Drake. Good luck with your daughter." As I walked away, I lifted my phone and put it to my ear. "Hi!" I fake answered.

"That was...strange," Ben said from beside me.

Keeping my eyes straight ahead, I nodded. "It sure was."

"He's watching you." I really wish Ben hadn't told

me that, because now I felt self-conscious, and whenever I felt self-conscious...sure enough, I tripped over a non-existent snag in the carpet, stumbled, and banged into the wall before finally righting myself. Way professional, Audrey. Ben barely noticed—it's not as if he hadn't seen me bumbling and stumbling around a million times before—he was busy watching Drake. "He's on his phone."

"His phone was on his desk," I pointed out.

"Well, he's picked it up to use it." Ben's sarcasm was not lost on me.

I shot him a look. "Okay, Hotshot," I drawled, "you said he's watching me. Is he still?" Ben nodded. "So that means he returned to his desk to retrieve the phone and is now standing in his doorway, I assume, talking on his phone and watching me."

Ben's grin was back. "You are so good at this. You should've joined the force with me, Audrey. I keep telling you, you're a natural."

"Wash your mouth out," I grumbled, affronted that he'd say such a thing.

"When are you going to get over this?" He sighed dramatically.

"When they issue a public apology. In print.

Preferably on the front page of the Firefly Bay Times," I shot back.

"That'll never happen."

"Exactly." We eventually reached the end of the longest hallway in the world and turned the corner, out of sight of Phillip Drake. "I wonder who he was calling?"

"And why?" Ben added.

"Do you think he's involved in your death?" We'd both gone over Ben's notes. It seemed like a pretty simple case. Find the dirt on Sophie Drake's boyfriend. It hadn't been difficult, yet Ben hadn't closed the case—and apparently hadn't forwarded the written report to Drake either. The question was, why? Drake had said Ben reported to him verbally the findings on Logan.

"Would you normally do that?" I asked.

"Do what?"

"Call in your report?"

"Sure, I'd give regular updates to my clients— they're the ones paying me after all. But at the end, I'd wrap it up with a written summary at the bare minimum."

I waved goodbye to Barbie as we crossed the foyer. "Where to next?" Ben asked.

I rummaged in my bag for the names I'd

scribbled on the back of an envelope. "Tonya Armstrong."

"Ah. The cheating spouse case."

"Whose husband, the cheater, is working for one Phillip Drake." My spidey senses were tingling. The two cases had to be connected—they just had to be. It was too much of a coincidence otherwise.

"Lead the way." Ben materialized himself into the passenger seat of my car while I took the more conventional route of unlocking the door before sliding in.

Tonya Armstrong lived with her husband at two seventy-eight Oakridge Circle. A nice, mid-level part of town. "I wonder if I should have spoken with her husband, Steven, while I was at the hotel," I said, barely paying attention to the traffic on the road.

"Speak with the client first," Ben gritted, hands gripping his seat, knuckles white.

"What? You already said it—you can't die again," I teased him, weaving in and out as I maneuvered my way through the busiest road in town before finally exiting onto Lexington. He visibly relaxed and laughed.

"Your driving always did give me heart palpitations, and apparently it's no different now I'm a ghost," he said drolly.

"Ha ha."

Within minutes I was pulling up in front of a perfectly ordinary house on a perfectly suburban street. I parked on the street, sparing the Armstrong's from my oil stains on their neatly paved driveway. A curtain twitched as I walked up the front path.

"Someone's definitely home," Ben said. "I'm going to duck ahead and check things out." I watched as he shot ahead and passed straight through the front door. I swear to God I will never get used to that. Tugging on the lapels of my jacket I continued on, rapping on the door. It swung open almost immediately.

"Yes?" A woman who looked about mid-thirties answered the door dressed in yoga pants and a wrinkled T-shirt.

"Tonya Armstrong?" I asked. She nodded. I launched into my spiel while she gripped the door and listened.

"I suppose you'd better come in," she said, turning away and leaving the door open for me to follow. I did. The house was immaculate inside, the furniture a little worn and outdated.

"Can I offer you a coffee?" Tonya asked, leading the way into the kitchen. "I'm having one," she added. Just in case I needed an incentive.

"That would be lovely, thank you." Ben hadn't reappeared and I could only guess that he was searching the house. For what I had no idea, but it was easier to talk to Tonya without him hovering over my shoulder.

"I'm sorry to hear about Ben," she said, busying herself with the coffee machine on the counter. "He seemed like a nice guy."

"He was." I nodded, feeling a lump form in my throat. I cleared my throat. "Would you mind quickly going through your case with me?" I asked. "Just so I can get everything squared away."

She puffed out a breath and tugged at the hem of her T-shirt. "Sure. So you probably read in my file that I hired him to follow my husband."

"Steven Armstrong," I read from the notes on my screen.

"Yes. I think he's having an affair." Her voice cracked, she swallowed, then continued, "I think he's been having an affair so I hired Ben to find out, one way or another."

"And did he?"

Tonya shot me a look I couldn't read. "He showed me some photos of Steven kissing another woman."

"So that's a yes." I nodded. I already knew this, of course. "So...case closed?" I prompted, knowing full well that it wasn't.

"I wanted more proof." She threw her hands up, tears filling her eyes as she blinked rapidly to dispel them. "I mean, what sort of fool am I, wanting even more proof that my husband is cheating on me?" she cried, wiping her nose on her sleeve. "I mean it was there, in the photos. It was definitely Steven, he was cupping this woman's face in his hands—he used to hold my face that way, a long time ago—and from the angle of the shot it was undeniable it was him. And there were more shots. Lots of them. Kissing. Intimately." A sob escaped, followed by another, then she was burying her face in her hands and howling. I had no idea what to do. Awkwardly I placed an arm around her shoulders, desperate for Ben to come back and give me some guidance. Of course, he didn't. He'd probably heard her crying and deliberately stayed away.

"I'm sorry about your husband," I said weakly.

She pulled away and gave me a watery smile. "Oh gosh, I'm so sorry, being all stupid and emotional," she apologized, grabbed a tissue from the box on the counter and blew her nose.

"It's not stupid at all," I assured her. "Having your

worst fears confirmed is the perfect time to be emotional."

"You're right." Tossing the tissue into the bin she straightened her shoulders and continued making the coffee. "I'm still not sure what I'm going to do," she said, back to me. "Steven doesn't know that I know. I assume he's still seeing her. Each time he's late home I know he's with her; each time he leaves the house on some errand I assume he's going to see her."

I grimaced, not knowing what to say. If it were me I'd dump his sorry ass. But it wasn't me. I wasn't married and I had no skin in this game.

"How long have you been married?" I asked instead, taking a seat at the kitchen table.

"Seven years." Then she snorted. "I guess the seven-year itch is a real thing, huh?"

"Umm. Ben said in his notes that you didn't believe him? When he told you Steven was, in fact, having an affair." I was reading the notes on my phone, almost jumped out of my skin when she placed a steaming cup of coffee in front of me. I hadn't heard her approach.

"Oh God. I was so awful to him." She sat down opposite me, cradling her own cup. "I'm afraid I got a little hysterical. Accused him of making it all up."

The blush of red in her cheeks showed her embarrassment was real.

"He didn't mention that here." I waggled my phone, trying to reassure her that he hadn't written down she was a hormonal overreactor.

"I thought the photos were staged, that he'd told Steven what he was doing and they pulled this prank on me, as revenge for me hiring a private investigator."

"Ben would never have been okay with anything like that," I assured her.

She had the grace to look ashamed. "I know. I'm afraid it was very much a case of shooting the messenger. I'd asked him to follow my husband—whom I suspected of having an affair—and if he was, to provide evidence of it. He did exactly that and I attacked him for it."

I took a sip of coffee, not knowing what to say. Tonya filled in the silence. "I'm a nurse, you see. I work a lot of night shifts. Sometimes we can go for a full week without physically crossing paths. I guess he got a little tired of that, of me not being here when he needed me."

I wanted to argue that none of this was her fault, but kept my mouth shut. I wasn't here as her friend. I was here as an investigator, and despite her distress,

I couldn't rule out that she was involved in Ben's death. What if she'd taken things further? What if she really blamed Ben for all of this, for shoving her husband's affair under her nose? Was it enough to tip her over the edge and kill him? Possibly.

"Witches are real," Brett Baxter told me. I sucked my lips, releasing them with a popping noise.

"Fair enough. You are entitled to believe whatever you want to believe." I nodded. I was in Brett's apartment. We'd finished up at Tonya Armstrong's. I'd bolted down my coffee and promised her an invoice would be hitting her inbox in the next day or so, making it very clear that as far as Delaney Investigations was concerned, her case was closed. She'd nodded, nose red, and thanked me for the visit. Then it was on to our third and final case. Brett had hired Ben to prove witches existed.

"You don't believe me," Brett huffed, crossing his arms over his chest.

I shook my head. "Not at all. It's just rather a broad statement and for a private investigator to actually investigate...you'd need something a little more specific than a generalized statement. What was it, exactly, that you wanted Delaney Investigations to do?"

Ben's notes had been maddeningly empty. Ben had written one word. Witch-hunt. I didn't know what that meant, and apparently neither did the ghost version of Ben. I was surprised that Ben had even agreed to take Brett on as a client. I figured it had to be the connection between the Armstrong case and the Phillips case, since Brett was the event planner for the Firefly Bay Hotel.

"Witches are real and they need to be wiped from this earth." Brett's voice was high with passion. My eyes swept his apartment, the decor in particular. Crosses hung on the walls, a huge painting of Jesus Christ hung on the wall above his television. Ben had disappeared like he had in Tonya's house—to see what I couldn't beyond the walls where I was currently standing. Having a ghost on my side was certainly coming in handy.

"And what makes you say that?" I asked, keeping my voice professional. It didn't matter what I

believed. Only what he'd hired Ben to investigate—
and if that was what led to Ben's death.

"Listen." Brett leaned in as if about to reveal a big
secret. "I'm the event planner at the Firefly Bay
Hotel." I nodded. Tell me something I don't know,
Brett. Thankfully he did. "So I hear things. A lot of
things." He tapped the side of his nose.

"Like what?" I pressed.

"Secrets," he whispered. You know, he presented as
a completely sane person. It was such a shame he was a
nutjob. Today was his day off, hence why we'd been
able to catch him at home. He was casually dressed in
blue jeans and a grey T-shirt, neatly pressed. His
brown hair was trimmed close at the sides, fashionably
coiffed on the crown of his head, and he had a neatly
trimmed beard. He looked around my age, give or
take. He also wore a very nice cologne and I had to
stop myself from leaning in to take a bigger whiff.

"I'm going to need something more...tangible," I
prodded. "You said Ben had accepted your case?
What exactly did he accept?" I pushed.

"Coffee?" Brett offered brightly, swiveling on his
heel and taking three steps into his kitchen. His
place was slightly bigger than mine in that his
bedroom wasn't in his living room and it appeared

he had a hallway. I never thought I'd have hallway envy, but here we were.

"Sure." Why not? A perk of the job I hadn't anticipated was free coffee. If all clients kept me caffeinated, I could be on a winner.

"So it's like this," Brett said, back to me while he prepared the drinks. "Like I said, I organize a lot of events. Like. A lot. And to make sure they run smoothly I attend each and every one, and that's how I discovered it. Snippets of conversations I'd pick up in passing, but over time...well, I started to keep a record."

I rolled my eyes. This guy was a nutso stalker. I wished Ben would hurry up and come back.

"I'm pretty sure they were having meetings. Of their coven."

"Their coven," I repeated.

"Yeah. Witches belong to covens. It was this same group of women, and I'd overhear them talking about witch stuff."

"Like what?"

"The moon. Crystals."

"Errr. Hardly proof that they're witches," I pointed out.

Brett shot me a glare over his shoulder. "I told you," he snapped. "I started keeping records."

"Okay?" I shrugged.

"Here." Brett thrust a steaming cup of coffee into my hand. "Lemme go get 'em." He shot out of the room and was back a couple of minutes later with an armful of journals, dumping them on the table. "Take a look," he offered. "You'll see."

Curious, I picked up a journal and flicked through it. Oh, good Lord. It was true. Brett had written down almost word for word snippets of conversations he'd overheard at events. I wasn't even sure that was ethical, as event planner for the hotel, that he was recording his guests. Well, sort of. Page after page of very neat handwriting.

"This is...impressive." I put the journal down.

"Thank you." Brett beamed, pleased with what he perceived to be praise.

"And did you tell Ben about these journals?" I asked.

Brett shook his head. "I hadn't had my first consult with Ben yet, other than to hire him, that is."

"And he accepted your case? That you wanted him to what? Prove that witches are real?" I really needed to get it clear in my head what Brett had wanted Ben to do for him.

"I wanted him to catch the witches," Brett said.

"Catch them?"

"In the act. Spellcasting and making blood sacrifices to further their own power." His face took on the same crazed look he'd had earlier.

"Right." I put my coffee cup down and was about to open my mouth to tell him we wouldn't be moving forward with his case when Ben strolled through the kitchen wall. I quirked a brow at him and he mimed talking on the phone.

"Oh, excuse me. My phone's vibrating," I said to Brett, pulling out my phone, pretending to swipe the screen and quickly holding it up to my ear before he could see the screen wasn't lit. "Delaney Investigations," I fake answered, wandering over to the living room window where Brett's apartment overlooked a parking lot.

"Don't ditch the case," Ben said.

"Why?"

"Because you're right. I think there's a connection with the Firefly Bay Hotel. I don't want you to cut him loose just yet."

"What sort of connection?" I lowered my voice. "What did you find?"

"Aside from all the religious artifacts he has scattered throughout the place, he's got all of the staff schedules pinned to his wall, with pins and strings linking them. Too bad I can't snap a photo for you."

"Yeah, that'd be handy. Any idea why?" Ben shook his head and I lapsed into silence while I mulled over what he'd told me. So Brett was what? Investigating his team members? And made a connection? I needed to get a look at the wall for myself. Ben's suggestion of a photo wasn't a silly one. If I could get access and snap a pic with my phone we'd be golden.

"You've had an idea." Ben grinned, hovering in front of me.

I nodded. "I have. Okay, thanks for the call." I wrapped up the fake call.

Turning back to Brett who was sitting at the table arranging the journals, I said, "Sorry about that. Would you mind if I used your bathroom?" It wasn't a lie. With all this coffee I did need to pee, but there'd be no time for indulging my bladder. I needed to get into Brett's bedroom, take a photo, and get out again. Preferably without him knowing.

"Sure. Door on the left." He waved toward the hallway. As I turned, my bag—that was still slung across my shoulder—swept across the table, collected my cup —still full of coffee—and sent the contents flying.

"Noooooo!" Brett screeched, trying to pull his

journals out of the path of the fast-flowing pool of coffee. It was too late for one poor journal that was now drenched. Jumping up, Brett grabbed a tea towel and began sopping up the mess.

"I'm so sorry."

He cut me a glare as he frantically tried to save his journals. "Just go use the bathroom," he snapped.

"Go," Ben urged. "This is going to keep him occupied for a few minutes. He won't notice how long you're gone. Brilliant plan."

"It wasn't intentional," I said out loud.

"I should hope not." Brett pouted, reminding me that I'd inadvertently spoken aloud to Ben. I really had to watch myself with that. This time I moved away more carefully, making sure my bag didn't knock anything else over.

I entered the bathroom, closed the door and turned on the cold water tap before carefully, slowly turning the knob and peeking my head outside. I could hear Brett in the living room, muttering about his journals and how they were ruined. I tiptoed to the door at the end of the hallway and wrapped my fingers around the handle, slowly turning. Thankfully he didn't have squeaky doors. I slipped inside and closed it behind me.

Ben was right. One wall contained what

appeared to be work schedules for staff members of the Firefly Bay Hotel. I snapped a dozen photos of the wall, plus other scraps of paper he'd pinned amongst the woven red thread that was connecting them all. Hurried to his desk that was also scattered with papers, snapped as many pictures as I dared before Ben popped his head through the door. "He's finishing up. Get out of here."

I hurried back to the bathroom, turned off the tap, a pang of guilt for wasting water, then rather noisily opened and closed the door behind myself and rejoined Brett in the living room where order had been restored.

"I'm so sorry," I offered again.

Brett, it seemed, had calmed down. "It's okay. They survived. The damage is minimal."

"That's good." I wiped my palms on my thighs. "I'll be honest with you, Brett. I'm not sure Delaney Investigations can help you. But"—I held up my hand when he opened his mouth to protest—"you paid a retainer and I will honor that. I'll look through the journals and see if I can find a pattern and then we'll talk again. Fair enough?"

Brett smiled. "I'm happy with that. How long, do you think?" He nodded toward the dozen journals he'd stacked on the table.

"How long will I need them?" I cocked my head, eyeballing the stack of reading I had in front of me. I wondered if Ben would be able to read them...if he could turn the pages, that is.

"Yeah." Brett wrung his hands. "I will need them back."

"Of course. Look, I'll take them with me today and get back to you next week. How does that sound?"

Brett was nodding. "Yes. Good. I can work with that."

Back in the car I tossed the journals that Brett had piled into a plastic shopping bag onto the back seat. Pulling away from the curb, I headed back to Ben's house. I'd visited all three of Ben's cases today and was still none the wiser as to who killed him.

13

I pulled up behind a familiar SUV parked out front of Ben's house. Climbing out of my car I watched while Detective Kade Galloway did the same, striding around his vehicle to meet me on the front lawn.

"Detective." I nodded my head in greeting, my eyes not missing the black jeans and blue checkered shirt. My heart fluttered at the sight. Why did my one weakness have to be currently adorning a cop? So unfair.

"Miss Fitzgerald." He nodded his head in greeting and I squinted, imagining him in a cowboy hat. Yep, that was all that was missing from my little fantasy.

"Call me Audrey," I said. "Only my bosses call me

Miss Fitzgerald and it's usually when I'm being fired."

"Bosses? As in...plural?"

I shrugged, leading the way up the garden path. "I'm a temp. Hence I have a lot of temporary bosses."

"Word on the street is you're now the owner of Delaney Investigations?" He rapped a knuckle on the sign that was attached to the wall by the front door.

"Word on the street?" I snorted. "You mean the Firefly Bay Police Department received the news that Ben's will has been read. I'm sure you have a copy of it and you're here now to see if I had motive for wanting my best friend dead." Sliding the key into the lock, the door swung open and I ushered him inside, not missing the hint of color in his cheeks. Yeah, that's why he was here all right.

"Almost, but no cigar," he said, coming to a halt in the living room and standing with hands on hips, legs planted. My eyes traveled the length of him, from the corded thighs to the chiseled chest and broad shoulders. His face was easy on the eyes too, the five o'clock shadow dusting a strong jaw, up to his stormy grey eyes that were currently giving me an equally thorough inspection. Heat rushed to my face and it was my turn to blush.

"Are you..?" Ben danced in front of me, peering

closely at my face. "You are!" he crowed. "You're blushing!" He laughed, then laughed some more. It was incredibly difficult to ignore him with Detective Galloway standing a few feet away. "Oh this is priceless." Ben's mirth continued unabated. "Audrey has the hots for a cop! If this doesn't take the cake!" He doubled over, holding his belly.

"Will you quit it?" I grumbled.

Galloway blinked in surprise. "Quit what?"

"Not you." I dismissed him with a wave of my hand and hurried toward the kitchen. *Distract him* was my one thought, or he was going to think I was an absolute loon.

"Who then?" he pressed, following me.

"I was talking to myself." I fiddled with the coffee machine like I knew what I was doing. Lord, but this thing was complicated. Why couldn't Ben have a simple old Keurig like I did? Pop in a pod and boom, you're done. "Coffee?" I offered, trying to get Ben's attention so he could do something useful like instruct me how to use the damn machine.

"Sure."

"Please." I indicated a stool at the breakfast bar. "Make yourself comfortable. Would you excuse me just one second?" My need for the bathroom hadn't been a lie at Brett Baxter's apartment and the need was becoming quite urgent. I clamped my knees together, concentrated on my kegels and shot off toward the guest bathroom without waiting for a reply.

Ben followed me in, but I shooed him out. "Seriously? I need to pee!" I whispered, waving my arms to shoo him back through the wall he'd appeared from. He must have been waiting outside, because as soon as he heard the toilet flush he was back.

"Jesus Christ, Ben," I complained, washing my hands, "can I not have two minutes to myself?"

"What? You're decent."

"And can you not cackle like a hyena when I have company?"

"I'm just sorry I didn't get to see this while I was alive," he replied with a grin.

"See what?"

"You. All flustered and fluttering your eyelashes at a man."

"I did not!" I protested.

He laughed. "Oh, you did. I have to admit, with all the boyfriends I've seen you with, I've never seen you act like this...with any of them. Maybe Galloway's the one."

"All the boyfriends?" I snorted. "You make it

sound like I've had hundreds. And Galloway is not the one."

"Ahhh, you are aware you treat boyfriends like your career? Temporary."

"What!" I was shocked. "I do not."

"Lemme see...never make plans beyond two weeks." He ticked off on one finger. "Never let them meet the family." He ticked off on another finger. "Never give them a drawer at your place—or vice versa." He paused in ticking the list off. "Actually I'm not sure you ever fully spent the night. Didn't you used to kick them out, no sleepovers?"

I narrowed my eyes, hating that he was right. "What? I don't sleep well with someone else in the bed." It was a weak excuse. The truth was, I'd never been the cuddling type. Sex? Yes, I liked it well enough, but snuggling afterward and falling asleep in each others arms? No, thanks. I ignored the rest of the points he'd made. So what if he was right? It didn't matter because Galloway was not my boyfriend.

By the time I returned from the bathroom, a steaming mug of coffee was waiting for me. I slid onto the barstool next to him.

"Thank you." I nodded toward my cup, beyond

relieved that I hadn't had to wrangle the complicated machine into submission.

"You're welcome. Do you always talk to yourself?" He took a sip of his brew, eyeballing me over the rim.

"Always." I shrugged. I knew he'd probably overheard me talking to Ben again at some point, no point in denying it.

"You were having quite the chat in the bathroom." Lucky for him he softened the words with a cute grin.

"I didn't think I was that loud." God, I hoped he hadn't heard what I'd actually said, and I frantically replayed the conversation with Ben in my mind to check for anything incriminating.

"Not at all. Just the murmur in the background."

I cleared my throat, studying the contents of my cup with great interest. "Yes. Well, just another one of my quirks."

"Ben didn't mention it. When talking about you," he clarified. "He said you were clumsy. And single."

"Pft. I didn't realize he needed to produce a dossier on me." The color was back in my cheeks; I could feel it burning like a sunburn.

"I actually wanted to talk to you about Ben. And offer you a deal," Galloway said, studying his cup.

"A deal?" I snorted. "I'm a suspect now that I've inherited all of this?" I waved my arm to indicate the room around us, narrowly missing hitting him. He instinctively ducked and I cringed. "Sorry," I muttered, mortified that I'd nearly smacked him in the face with the back of my hand.

He straightened and grinned at me. "You certainly know how to keep a guy on his toes!"

I heard Ben's muffled guffaw from behind me and narrowed my eyes in warning. Then Galloway's words penetrated. Was he flirting? I focused on him again. I couldn't tell.

"To answer your question, no, you're not a suspect," he assured me.

"Oh? Why not?" Oh my God Audrey, shut up! Quit while you're ahead girl.

"Your alibi checked out." He shrugged.

"My alibi?" I didn't remember giving him one.

"The coroner put Ben's death between ten and eleven p.m. on Wednesday night. Multiple witnesses already put your whereabouts at the Crown & Anchor, and we have CCTV footage of you leaving after midnight."

"Ahhhh." I nodded. "That's good then."

"Actually I dropped by because Ben was going to give me a file."

"A file? What, on one of his cases?" I'd seen Ben's cases and none of them were that interesting—not interesting enough that a police detective would want a copy.

"I can't say."

I peered at him incredulously. "You can't say? Then how do I know what it is you want? That's if I decide to give it to you, which I'm not convinced is the right course of action."

"I just need access to his computer—I'll find it myself."

I crossed my arms, shaking my head. "No way. Not going to happen."

"You don't know it yet, but you've got a problem," he said. I narrowed my eyes, praying he wasn't a dirty cop like some of his co-workers, because I was really worried that what he was going to say next would constitute blackmail.

Galloway continued. "In order for you to continue Ben's business, you're going to need a Private Investigators license."

"That's a thing?" I was surprised. I'd never really asked Ben about that side of things. I'd always figured that if you just decided you liked solving mysteries you'd hang out your shingle and boom, you're in business.

"It is. It was pretty simple for Ben. He automatically qualified since his years on the force counted toward the criteria. But you, on the other hand..." He drifted off, leaving me to fill in the blanks.

"I've got zero experience in law enforcement. Or investigative work. Okay, well I can fix that, what do I need to do?"

Galloway reached into his back pocket and pulled out a folded sheet of paper and handed it to me. I read it, my heart sinking with each line. Not only did I have to go to PI school, I needed twelve hundred supervised work experience hours. Not to mention passing an exam. My heart sank even further. Not only did I not have anyone who could supervise me, but it would also mean moving away from Firefly Bay while I completed my studies and got my qualifications.

My shoulders slumped.

"I can help you with that," Galloway said, intruding on my thoughts. I looked at him dejectedly. "You can get the college credits via distance education. And I'm prepared to be your supervisor," he added.

I blinked in shock. That was a pretty big commitment on his behalf.

"In exchange for what?"

"I need that file."

"The one Ben said he'd give you?"

Galloway nodded.

"You could just subpoena Ben's files," I pointed out, spinning my cup in my hands, wondering why I was hesitating and not jumping all over his offer. This would solve all my problems. But it also meant I'd be committing to twelve hundred hours in his company. A double-edged sword if ever there was one.

"I could do that," he agreed. "But if we go down that road, I'd be subpoenaing everything. The entire contents of his office. Is that what you want me to do?"

My cup wobbled and I almost spilled the contents. I steadied it with both hands and quit fiddling with it. "Actually that would be a pain," I admitted. "I kinda need his stuff." For despite what he'd just told me about me not being legally qualified to be a PI, I still had every intention of investigating Ben's death. Oh, and closing the cases he'd been working on.

He grinned again. "That's what I thought. So in the interests of strengthening relations between the force and Delaney Investigations I propose to you the same deal I offered Ben with some minor adjustments. You give me access to Ben's files and I'll teach you how to be a private investigator."

Ben was being suspiciously quiet in all of this. Usually, he didn't shut up, but now, when I could really use his input, he remained annoyingly silent. I wanted to twist around and look at him over my shoulder so badly, but that would look super weird. Instead, I kept my gaze on Galloway, ignoring the cold presence at my back, knowing Ben was hovering there, as intrigued as I was by Galloway's offer.

"Take it," Ben whispered, making me jump. Yes, I'd known he was there. I just hadn't expected him to speak directly into my ear.

Galloway noticed me jerk but didn't say anything, just waited for my response, sipped his coffee as if he had all the time in the world.

"This isn't illegal, is it?" Because it reeked of underhanded subterfuge.

"It is not. But it is classified. And I will need you to not say a word about it. To anyone."

Narrowing my eyes, I studied him. "Okay, I'll give you access to his files on one condition."

His eyebrows rose. "I hardly think you're in a position to negotiate."

Ha. He didn't know me at all. Just because I was clumsy didn't make me stupid. "That's where you're wrong. Sure, you can subpoena Ben's files. But that's going to take time and you'd need a judge to sign off on it. You could probably swing it as part of his murder investigation—that'd speed things along. But you and I both know you met with Ben before he was killed, so whatever it is you're looking for isn't related to his death. Not directly. Also, you want this kept quiet, so I doubt you're prepared to subpoena his files. Your offer to help me with PI training is tempting, I admit, but I have other options in that regard too." I could move to the city for the duration of my training. It wasn't ideal but it wasn't out of the question either. Or I could nix the whole thing and close Delaney Investigations. A little piece of my heart shriveled at the thought.

He regarded me silently for a full minute. I swallowed and tried not to be intimidated. "What are you proposing?" he ground out.

"It's simple really. You tell me what this is about."

"Not going to happen."

"Then no deal."

"Audrey," Ben warned. I shot him a glare. He didn't remember what he'd been doing before he died, he didn't remember his cases, he sure as hell didn't remember what sort of deal he had going on with Galloway. And if Galloway wasn't going to tell me, then I wasn't going to play ball, pure and simple.

"You've got balls, I give you that," Galloway said, a hint of admiration in his voice.

"Well yes, only mine are on the inside." I nodded in agreement.

Galloway blew out a sigh, his face resigned. "Okay. But this goes no further. I'm taking a huge risk telling you and I cannot afford to have word of this getting out." He glanced up at the ceiling and muttered something to himself about pushy women.

I couldn't believe he'd caved. I'd fully expected him to leave without either of us getting what we wanted. Of course, now that he had, I had a twinge of concern that maybe I didn't want to know this big bad secret. What if it's what got Ben killed? Would it put a target on my back too? Although to be fair, any of his cases could be behind his murder and I may already be a target.

"You're overthinking," Ben whispered near my ear. I lowered my head and willed my brain to stop spinning. It didn't.

"I'm part of an undercover task force," Galloway said, voice devoid of emotion. "To investigate—and put a stop to—corruption in the force."

My head snapped up. "You should have led with that," I told him.

"So you know about Ben's case?"

I snorted. "Of course I know what those assholes did to him. I'm his best friend. I was by his side throughout the entire debacle. I saw what it did to him!" I poked Galloway in the chest, hard. "Why has it taken this long, huh? Three years. That's a pretty shitty response time."

Galloway had the grace to look remorseful. "The task force was only created this year. As I said, it's undercover. Secret. We can't have anyone finding out about it; otherwise they'll go into hiding and we'll never catch them at it."

"By them, you mean cops? Your fellow officers?" I needed to be one hundred percent certain clear we were on the same page. Galloway nodded.

"What if this is some trick? Get me to hand over all of Ben's proof that Firefly Bay Police Department is corrupt, then you destroy it and it was all for nothing."

"All I can give you is my word." Galloway shrugged. It was true. There were no guarantees I could trust him. There was a time when I would trust virtually anyone, but those days were gone. The department had nearly destroyed Ben. They'd kicked him while he was down. Not only had he been dealing with his father's illness and the heartbreaking decision to put him into care, but they framed him as a bad cop. Falsified reports, tampered with evidence. They'd left him with no option. Be fired for misconduct or resign. All because he'd witnessed a payoff between an officer and a drug dealer.

"You've been in Firefly Bay a while. Why now?"

He looked puzzled. "I'm not sure I know what you mean? Yes, I've been here for two years. But the task force has only recently been formed."

"And no one in the Firefly Bay Police Department is involved in the task force? Just you?"

He inclined his head. "Just me." Then he elaborated, "The task force is statewide. Firefly Bay isn't the only station with problems, hence, the task force."

I chewed my lip. He could be spinning me total bullshit. "I believe him," Ben said. My most troubling thought was that I did too. I didn't want to—every fiber of my being was protesting—but my gut instinct told me Galloway was on the up-and-up. "Fitz, if we can stop the corruption that we both know is happening then we have to trust him. We have to take the chance." I liked how Ben said *we*. That I wasn't alone in this, he had my back.

I nodded my head. Once. "What is it you need?"

"Ben said he kept his own reports of everything that happened. That's what we were meeting about the day we bumped into you. I'd reached out to him, we had a conversation and he told me everything he knew."

"You know it was Ian Mills Ben saw, accepting a bribe from a drug dealer he was meant to be arresting?"

Galloway nodded. "I do. I'm also looking at Sergeant Dwight Clements and Deputy Police Chief James Clarke." I wasn't surprised to hear Dwight's name come up, he and Ian were as thick as thieves, both on duty and off. James Clarke surprised me, but then I figured someone high up in the department had to be involved; otherwise things would never have escalated as they did. "Remember," Galloway added, "not a word. This is strictly between us."

"Oh good. You're back. Feed me." Thor burst through the cat door and sat next to his temporary food bowl.

"You've still got food in there," I told him, pointing out the obvious.

"I can see the bottom!" Thor's outrage was real.

"Fine, fine." I slid off the barstool, scooped a measure of kibble from the pantry and topped up his bowl. "Happy now?" I asked.

He ignored me, the only sound the crunch of kibble between his teeth. And then I looked up and caught the amused expression on Galloway's face. Holy heck I'd forgotten only I could understand Thor—so now Galloway thought I spent half my time talking to myself and half my time talking to Ben's cat. Why he hadn't run for the hills was beyond me. Surely he must think I'm an absolute looney tune by now. But he didn't say anything and I decided if he could ignore the fact that I was having conversations with a cat, so could I.

"You'd better follow me," I told him, jerking my head toward Ben's study.

14

*D*etective Galloway opened his mouth to speak when a loud "Yoohoo!" came from the sliding door behind him, followed by a tapping noise. Over his shoulder, I saw Mrs. Hill waving at me through the glass.

"Sorry," I muttered through gritted teeth. "You've met the neighbor, Mrs. Hill?" I asked as I breezed past on my way to the door.

"Indeed." I'm pretty sure I heard a hint of humor in his voice, but I couldn't be one hundred percent sure.

Flicking the latch on the door, I slid it open, moving my body to block her entrance. Only I wasn't fast enough and she brushed past me with a sharp nudge of her elbow. "Ow," I muttered, rubbing my rib cage and eyeballing the hellion from next door.

"Can I help you, Mrs. Hill?" I asked with forced politeness. She was in another floral dress, her hand twisting the pearls around her neck.

"I was wondering what you were doing here," she replied, not taking her eyes off of Galloway who had stood at her entrance, giving her a little nod.

"Feeding Thor." I glanced down at the grey cat who hadn't lifted his head from his bowl. "Who's going to get fat at this rate," I added.

"Hey!" he grumbled. "Back off. I've had a trauma. I'm comfort eating."

Mrs. Hill sniffed. "Yes. Well. You told me that before. I just don't think it's appropriate that you're here at all."

Galloway didn't miss my eye roll, not by the way his lips twitched.

"Yes well, I have some news for you on that front, Mrs. Hill." Oh, I was going to enjoy this—and for a nanosecond I felt bad about it, but that feeling soon vanished. Mrs. Hill gave me nothing but grief and it was clear as the nose on my face that she didn't like me. She was going to like what I had to tell her next even less.

"I'm your new neighbor!" I announced, rocking

back on my heels, a fake smile plastered on my face as I watched her reaction. As anticipated she couldn't hide it. She did a good job of trying to, but I was watching for those telltale signs I knew so well. The flaring of her nostrils, the stiffening of her spine, the way her tongue shot out to touch her upper lip. All signs that she was pissed off. Usually at me. There was something about my mere presence that got on her nerves, and despite me trying on countless occasions to befriend her, we'd never gotten past me being that annoying friend of Ben's. The one that wasn't good enough.

"What do you mean?" Her voice came out three octaves higher than usual and the hand that had been fiddling with her pearls, clutched them in a death grip so tight I feared they'd break and scatter across the floor.

I made sure my following words were not as gleeful as they sounded in my head, hoping I was injecting just enough somber introspection into them. "Ben left me his house in his will," I explained. "Actually he left me everything."

You could have heard a pin drop. Well, you could have if Thor would stop crunching the damn kibble. Instead, his noisy little jaws continued to work away, *crunch, crunch, crunch*, as Mrs. Hill stood ramrod straight, a look of utter disbelief on her face. Then she left. Without a word. She simply walked out, leaving the door open in her wake. I pulled a face and slid it closed.

"That was odd." Galloway said.

I sagged with relief. "Oh good, you think so too? Because sometimes with her I think it's just me."

"Ugh, yeah." He nodded, his gaze thoughtful as he looked toward the gate in the fence separating the properties, the one Mrs. Hill had just disappeared through. I could faintly hear Percy barking in the distance.

"I'm predicting she'll make herself a nice cup of tea, calm down, and then be back with a million questions laced with disdain about how Ben could be friends with someone like me, let alone leave me all his possessions."

"She seemed really shocked about that." Galloway was still looking at the gate.

"I'm going to check on her," Ben said. He'd been quiet for so long that I'd actually forgotten he was with us.

"Sure." I shrugged, then caught the sharp look Galloway darted my way. Damn it. Busted talking to a ghost. Again. I scrambled to cover my ass. "I mean, she sure did. Anyway..." I clapped my hands together. "Back to business. Follow me."

He did. I sat at Ben's desk, jiggled the mouse to wake up the computer and typed in the password.

"You know his passwords?" Galloway asked, dragging up the old wooden chair from the corner and making himself comfortable by my side.

"Uh-huh." I nodded, fingers flying over the keyboard. "I set up most of his systems."

"Did you help him with recording his case?"

I ground my teeth, remembering it oh so well. Ben had been preparing to go to internal affairs, blow the whistle on Mills, when an assault charge had been laid on him. He'd arrested a guy, one of the street thugs for vehicular theft, only that thug had claimed excessive force and was suddenly sporting a black eye. A black eye he hadn't had when Ben brought him in.

"I set up a spreadsheet for him to track things, yes." I pulled up the spreadsheet in question, leaning back in my chair while Galloway leaned forward to read the screen.

"This is very detailed. Very thorough." I wasn't sure if Galloway was talking to himself or me. I may have set up the spreadsheet, but Ben had entered the information. Every precise detail. Dates, times, every exchange, he recorded it. He had photos too. He'd had the sense to snap a photo with his mobile of anything and everything that tied the corruption back to Mills. What I hadn't known, and I assume Ben hadn't known either, was how high up in the department it went—he had no evidence to support Galloway's theory on Deputy Police Chief Clarke being dirty.

Opening a drawer, I pulled out a blank USB. Ben kept a stash to give copies of surveillance footage to his clients. Inserting the USB I copied the spreadsheet over, and the dozens of photos. Each photo's file path was recorded in the spreadsheet.

"This is helpful. Very helpful." Galloway nodded, clearly pleased. I ejected the USB and handed it to him. He took it, looked me dead in the eye and said, "Thank you. I know it doesn't mean much to you now, but this will help clear Ben's name." He stood and returned the chair to its spot in the corner. I followed him back into the living room.

"That's where you're wrong. It means a hell of a lot to me. That's why I'm taking a chance that I can trust you," I shot back. "Am I in danger? If Mills, Clements and Clarke catch wind of what you're up to, will it lead back to me? Do I have a target on my back?" Then another, more chilling thought occurred to me. "Did one of them kill Ben? Did they already know? Is this why he died?"

Galloway shrugged. "Until we find who killed Ben and why, I can't say. We're assuming it's related to one of his cases, but one thing about police work is you never make assumptions. You need evidence to back it up."

"That's not comforting," I said.

"Wasn't meant to be," he shot back. "Ben and I were discreet. We met walking along the street. To anyone else it would have looked like a casual conversation as we walked from one end of the block to the other. It had to be that way to avoid any suspicion. So no, I'm highly doubtful it was Mills or Clements. And Clarke wouldn't get his fingers dirty. He's pulling the strings from higher up."

"Right." My initial enthusiasm for the PI field dimmed just a little. I'd been excited about taking over Ben's business, of seeing myself as a super sleuth private investigator. But now I may have just put a massive target on my back.

"I'm telling you this so you can take precautions. Be mindful of your own safety. There's no reason to think that you're next."

I nodded. Heaven help us all if this got me killed, I'd be really pissed with him.

Ben returned with a gust of arctic air. "That's odd," he commented.

Galloway was at the sink rinsing his cup so I mouthed the word "Oh?" to Ben while jerking my head toward the detective.

Ben gave Galloway a glance and then slid onto the barstool the other man had recently vacated. "I couldn't get into Ethel's house," he answered.

"What?" That got my attention. Ben could move through walls—how could he not get into her house?

"What?" Galloway said over his shoulder. "Did you say something?" Turning off the tap, he grabbed a tea towel and dried off his cup before returning it to its rightful place—the cupboard above the coffee machine. God, he was even house trained. He'd be perfect if it weren't for that one major defect. He was a cop. I sighed wistfully. Such a waste.

"Audrey?" he prompted when I didn't reply and I suspected I was eyeballing him with a rather dreamy expression on my face, for that grin was back, the one with the endearing dimple that was oh, so distracting.

"Nope, didn't say a word," I lied. Lies were falling thick and fast from my lips these days and I wondered if I should be worried about that. After all, we grow up being told lying is bad, yet here I was, dispensing them like candy on Halloween. For the greater good, I assured myself.

"I wonder where you go," Galloway said, more to himself than me.

"Hmmmm?" I arched a brow, still half lost in thought.

His grin widened, showing even, white teeth. He had very nice teeth I noticed, running my tongue over my own. My bottom teeth were crooked and I'd thought about having work done to straighten them, but all of that cost money that I didn't have. Correction, money that I didn't used to have. But now I did. Maybe I should make an appointment with my dentist.

"In that head of yours. I wonder where you go. You drift off, your mind miles away." He'd folded his arms across his chest and leaned back against the kitchen cupboard looking all sexy cowboy—minus the hat—and hot detective. My ovaries were having a hard time keeping their minds on the job—and that was finding Ben's killer. The mental reminder was enough to snap me out of my fantasizing.

15

I was keen to get started on my PI school application, but two things happened. My phone rang and so did Galloway's.

Peering through the crack on the screen, I sighed. I couldn't ignore this one.

"Mom!" I answered, hearing Galloway barking into his own phone, clearly not happy with whoever was on the other end.

"Audrey, love, how are you?" Mom's voice was all sympathy and warm hugs and I sagged a little, a sudden yearning to be wrapped in her arms, to rest my head on her shoulder.

"I'm okay," I said. And I was. Sort of. I didn't know how I'd be coping if Ben weren't around in ghost form, but I was adjusting reasonably fast to my new normal. Of course, I couldn't tell her that.

"Darling, you don't have to lie to me. I'm your mother. And Ben was your best friend. Gosh, I can't remember a time when the two of you weren't joined at the hip." She went off on a trip down memory lane and I smiled, my eyes misty. Ben and I sure had racked up a lot of memories. I tuned back in, catching the tail end. "...need help with?"

I looked around at the mess the police had left Ben's house in and on a whim suggested a cleaning party.

"We can certainly do that," Mom agreed and I realized she was grieving too. Ben was another son to her. And having something tangible to do helped.

"Remember, Mom, earth-friendly products. Actually Ben probably has everything he needs here."

"Here? You're at Ben's house?"

"Oh, yeah. Sorry, I should've called you, but it's been hectic. Ben left me everything in his will. His lawyer called me into his office today."

"Oh!" It was one of those things that came as a shock, but then when you took a minute and thought about it, it made perfect sense. Which was exactly what mom said. "That makes sense." I could visualize her on the other end of the phone, nodding. "I know your dad, Laura and Dustin would like to help too," she said.

"Sure. Everyone is welcome. It'll be nice to get this place cleaned up. Ben would hate to see it like this and it would take me hours on my own."

"It's not...there's not..." Mom trailed off and I frowned before realizing what she was asking. She was worried there might be blood.

I shook my head. "Nothing like that, Mom. Just fingerprint dust and they've pulled stuff out of cupboards that needs putting away, that's all."

"Good, good. Well, I'll rally the troops."

"See you soon." We said our goodbyes and hung up. Galloway had finished his call and was standing a few feet away waiting for me to finish mine.

"Sounds like you have plans," he said.

I nodded. "Family is coming over. We're having a cleaning bee." I waved my hand at the disarray around us.

"Good. Well." He held out his hand to shake mine and I automatically took it. His grip was firm and warm, and my hand was dwarfed in his. "Thanks for your help. I'll hold up my end of the bargain, but in the meantime get yourself enrolled in PI school. There will be paperwork I'll have to sign to confirm I'll be your supervisor."

"Right. Will do." I didn't know why we were awkward with each other, but to say we were was an understatement. I walked him to the door, leaning back against it after he'd left, wondering if I'd just made a colossal mistake.

"What's up?" Ben asked, hovering in front of me.

"Am I making a mistake trusting him?" I asked, chewing a nail.

"Who, Kade?" Ben sounded surprised. "Absolutely not. He's one of the good guys, Audrey. Hell, do you think I'd have left you alone with him if I didn't trust him?"

"Pft. Like you could have done anything if he'd attacked me." I mean, really! Ben was incorporeal. He couldn't touch a thing, let alone help me if someone was out to hurt me.

"That's not the point." He huffed. "The point is, you can trust him. You have nothing to worry about from Kade Galloway."

The sun was dipping over the horizon, the sky a riot of reds, oranges, and pinks.

"Corker of a sunset," Dad said, lowering himself

to sit next to me on the edge of the deck, my one-year-old niece Isabelle cradled on his lap.

"It sure is." I smiled at Dad. "Thanks for helping today." My family had been amazing. Everyone had turned up. Brad, Dustin, and Amanda had come straight from work, Dustin wrangling Madeline and Nathaniel from daycare. The kids had stopped their whining at leaving the funnest place on earth as soon as they'd spotted their favorite aunty and had immediately set to playing on the back lawn while the adults got busy inside. Except for me. I'd been shooed out the back door and designated babysitting duty, which was honestly no hardship at all. Ben had been agitated to begin with, having his belongings touched by other people. Just the thought of it had him all twitchy until I eventually muttered under my breath to calm down. He had. He'd taken a breath and then sat down by my side—thankfully the opposite side to Dad; otherwise Dad would have sat right on top of him. Or in him. Eeeew.

"This is what family does," Dad said. "I'm sorry about Ben." Dad patted my back, voice gruff.

"Yeah. Me too." I sighed. This was hard, being around sad people was making me sad. And I should be sad. It was only right that I was, but I was the lucky one—I had the ghost version of Ben right by my side and I'd take that over no Ben at all, any day.

"Pizza's here!" Mom called from the doorway. Madeline, a three-year-old after my own heart, immediately dropped the ball she'd been playing with and moved at lightning speed across the lawn, elbowing her way between me and Dad to get to the pizza. Her little brother Nathaniel toddled after her. I scooped him up and propped him on my hip while Dad carried Isabelle inside.

Laura had spread a checkered tablecloth on the floor and Madeline was already sitting on it, pizza in hand, a look of delight on her face at the impromptu indoor picnic.

"Good idea." I sat Nathaniel next to his cousin and Mom handed over a bite-sized piece of pizza for him, which he immediately shoved into his mouth. Isabelle was next, she'd already managed to snag pizza before Dad had even sat her on the tablecloth and I chuckled at her passion for food. They were good kids, and I loved being around them. I ignored the ache in my ovaries that reminded me that time was passing and if I wanted this for myself...well, I didn't want babies bad enough to settle down with the wrong man. And that was the problem.

According to Ben, anyway. Apparently I was too choosy. Personally I didn't think that was a bad thing.

"You okay there, Audrey?" My brother, Dustin, nudged my shoulder and I realized I'd been daydreaming.

I shook myself out of it. "Yep. All good."

Sitting around Ben's dining table, two massive pizza's spread out between us, we ate. There was teasing, laughter and love. Naturally I spilled my drink. It was a given. Mom had been ready with the paper towels and I looked across the table, where Ben was standing behind my dad's left shoulder, laughing along with the rest of them.

"Awwww geez, Fitz." Ben sobered, noticing the misty look in my eyes. "Don't. Don't get all sad on me."

"Sorry," I whispered, sniffing and blinking rapidly to dispel the moisture.

My big sister, Laura, who was sitting on my right, slung an arm around my shoulders and squeezed. "No need to apologize, Aud. I know some people give you a hard time about being clumsy"—she shot a sharp look at my sister-in-law, Amanda— "but it's what makes you uniquely you. And we wouldn't have you any other way."

Before I knew it, they were all raising their glasses and giving clumsy Audrey a toast.

"Oh good, pizza!" Thor busted through the cat door and made a beeline for the three children sitting on the floor, discarded pieces of pizza scattered around them.

"Thor," I warned. "You really shouldn't be eating people food. It's not good for you."

"Why not?" he replied, mouth full. "It's so delicious." He actually started purring as he ate and I laughed out loud when Thor, who usually made himself scarce whenever my nieces and nephews were around, tolerated the rough pats and cuddles all three bestowed on him while he stole their pizza.

"You're incorrigible." I sighed, knowing the kids would riot if I pulled the cat away. Dustin had whipped out his phone and began snapping pictures.

"So I hear you inherited Ben's estate?" Amanda said. It was a rhetorical question because I knew Mom would have told them all already, so I nodded, eyes sweeping over her. Despite the fact that she'd been at work all day she looked immaculate. She'd slipped off her jacket and shoes, but still, in her pencil skirt and white blouse she looked crisp and fresh and I knew if our positions were reversed I'd be a mess by now. I'd have various stains on the shirt and my hair wouldn't be that dead straight waterfall that looked like it had never been ruffled in its life; instead it would be a beehive, with strands sticking out every which way. I sighed. I really needed to stop comparing myself to Amanda.

"I did."

"What's the plan?" she asked next. "Are you going to sell?"

"Sell?!" I was taken aback. "Of course not." Geez, I would never sell Ben's home.

"You could make a very good profit—after taxes of course—and buy something nicer. Beasley, Tate and Associates are available to assist with any estate planning needs you may have," she offered. I knew she meant to be helpful, but holy heck. We hadn't even buried Ben yet and she was thinking about liquidating his assets.

"Amanda!" Dustin snapped, glaring at her. "Now's not the time. Or the place. For Christ's sake."

"Oh. Sorry." Amanda shrugged and I wondered, not for the first time, if she was somewhere on the Autism Spectrum.

"Babe, you okay?" Brad, Laura's husband, the quiet one of the bunch who you often forget was around because he was that quiet, peered at his wife who had her face buried in her hands.

"Laura?" I joined him in my concern. Her shoulders were shaking and I wasn't sure if she was crying or laughing. God, I hoped it was laughing. For if Laura started crying then I was going to follow and I'd been holding myself together pretty well. It would be a shame to come unraveled at this point. She dropped her hands, lifted her face, and despite her cheeks being wet, they were tears of laughter. I sagged in relief. "What's so funny?" I asked.

Laura waved at Amanda, choked on her words, and peeled into streams of laughter again. We all looked on, a little puzzled, but her giggles were infectious and pretty soon the whole table was laughing with no idea why. Eventually, we sobered, pulling ourselves together, cheeks wet from tears. It actually felt really good to laugh like that, very cathartic.

Even uptight Amanda had laughed with us. "Okay, but seriously, what's the plan, Audrey?"

"Considering I only found out about it this afternoon? I haven't planned anything. But I won't be selling," I hastened to add. "I am taking over Ben's business though."

"Oh, that's wonderful." Mom clapped, then glanced at Dad. "Isn't it?"

But Dad was nodding. "I could see you in the

investigative line of work. Always said to Ben you'd make a good partner."

"You did?" That was a surprise. I didn't know Dad had told Ben that.

"You've got a very sharp, very inquisitive mind." Ben had said those exact words to me.

My smile was wide and my chest puffed out with pride. "Thank you." I sighed and took a sip of my wine. "I've got to go to PI school though. Apparently you need a license to be an investigator."

"And insurance," Amanda added. Of course, she'd know.

"Sure. All of those things." I shrugged.

"School? Does that mean you have to move away?"

"Nope. I'd been worried about that too, but I can study online as long as I have a supervisor."

"But who will supervise you?" Laura asked.

"Detective Galloway." I saw the way they all exchanged looks. It was no secret how I felt about law enforcement.

"Oh, he's lovely." Amanda nodded in apparent approval. "Very nice to look at too." And then she winked at me. Winked! Okay, we were definitely in some sort of alternate universe.

"You know him?" Laura asked her.

"He's been into work a time or two." She shrugged. "Always friendly, polite, professional."

"Now I've gotta look this guy up," Laura muttered, pulling out her phone, and bringing up the Facebook app, she began stalking. It didn't take long. She let out a wolf whistle. "Oh, Audrey Fitzgerald, you sly dog. Trust you to choose the hottest guy in the Firefly Bay Police force." She nudged me with her elbow.

"I didn't choose him," I protested, feeling my cheeks heat. "He chose me." Oh God, that sounded worse. After another round of teasing had subsided, I said, "He's the detective investigating Ben's murder. He did me a solid by explaining how the licensing works and that if I wanted to run Ben's business, I'd need to become a qualified investigator. He offered to help. End of story." Sort of. I left out the part how he was part of a secret task force to take down certain members of the Firefly Bay Police Department.

"Which reminds me," I continued, "while I have you here—I'm going to need help planning Ben's funeral. As soon as his body is released by the coroner I'm going to have the funeral home on the phone and I've got no idea what to do."

I should have known Mom would be all over it.

She rummaged in her bag and slapped a notebook on the table, flipped it open to a page already filled with notes, or, —I squinted to get a better look— questions, it seemed. Casket? Burial or cremation? I was glad I had them here to help, but we were going to need a whole lot more wine.

As if I'd magicked it up by my thoughts alone, another bottle of red appeared in front of me. Brad smiled and patted my shoulder. "You look like you could use this," was all he said.

16

*G*roaning, I reached out an arm, felt around on the nightstand for my phone, managed to grab it before I knocked it to the floor, then managed to catapult it into my forehead. Again. This morning just smacks of deja vu.

"You have got to be kidding me." Cracking open an eye, I peered at the window. The blind was down, but light was peeking in around the edges. Okay, that was a start. Now to ascertain how early or late in the day it was. Sitting up, I swung my legs out of bed, then balanced on the edge of my mattress for a minute until the room had stopped spinning.

"Oh good, you're awake." Ben's gratingly cheerful voice reached my ears. I glanced up to see him sitting on my kitchen bench.

"Whaaaa?" I grumbled. "What happened?"

He chuckled. "You and a bottle of red wine."

Right. I remembered that. We'd been planning his funeral. Urgh, I still didn't want to think about it. Standing up, I hurried into the bathroom, waved a hand at Ben and instructed him to "stay there." For once, he obeyed and was still sitting on the kitchen bench when I returned.

"Brad drove you home in your car. You didn't want to stay at my place." There was a tone in his voice. I cocked my head trying to identify it. Hurt? Annoyed?

"I didn't want to stay at your house...without you." My own voice sounded pitiful to my own ears. "It's strange there without you—and I know you're here, but you're not, not really. And I need time to adjust. So yeah, I didn't want to wake up in that house alone." I blurted. Of course, I knew I'd have to, eventually. It didn't make sense for me to keep my apartment and Ben's house, and let's face it, his place is a million times nicer than my shoebox.

"Oh."

"Did I hurt your feelings?" I asked.

"I didn't think so, not initially, but now you've explained that...yeah...I think my feelings were a little hurt," he admitted.

I eyeballed him. "Toughen up, princess."

His head tipped back and he laughed. "Thought I had you there for a minute." He chuckled.

"Nice try." Gathering up my clothes, I headed into the bathroom, stood under the shower and remembered Ben's guest bathroom and the non-stop hot water. Not the on again, off again disaster of my current bathroom. The thought of moving was becoming more and more appealing, I just wasn't quite ready...yet.

Coming out of the bathroom, I searched for my phone. After it had bounced off my forehead I'd lost track of it. Eventually, I found it under the bed, only to discover it had two percent battery left. Sitting back on my haunches, I stared up at the ceiling, having one of those why me moments. A headache was thrumming away behind my eyeballs and I badly —badly—needed coffee. I crawled to my nightstand and reached for the power cord only to find it missing. Rising up to my knees I looked all around, but the damn thing was gone. "You have got to be kidding me." I swear there's an alternate universe where all of my pens, hair clips, earrings, and phone cords live. How could I have possibly lost it when it had been plugged into the wall next to my bed?

"You took it with you yesterday," Ben offered up,

"shoved it in your bag in case your phone went flat. Said something about it not holding its charge these days?"

"Oh. Right." I sat back on my haunches and tried to remember, had a vague recollection. Spying my bag on the sofa, I dug through it and sure enough, there was my power cord. With my phone finally charging, I headed to my Keurig, opened the overhead cupboard to grab a pod, only my hand met emptiness.

"Noooooo!" I wailed, hand flailing around as I searched for a pod. Standing on tiptoe, I peered into the cupboard. No pods. "There are no pods," I whispered, voice bordering on hysterical. "No. Pods."

"Better call a state of emergency," Ben teased.

I rounded on him. "It's okay for you, you don't need coffee anymore. I need coffee. I cannot function without coffee."

"Okay, okay, calm down," he soothed, sliding off the counter. "We'll go out for coffee. You need to drop by my place and check on Thor anyway. We can get coffee on the way."

Oh my god, I'd forgotten about Thor. I hadn't even noticed he wasn't here. I was a shit pet parent. Ben burst out laughing. "You might have some explaining to do with your family."

"Did I talk to Thor in front of them?" I bet I had. "Or more precisely, did Thor and I have a conversation in front of them?"

Ben nodded. "If it's any consolation, they were quite entertained as the two of you argued, only of course all they could hear from Thor was various meows and odd little noises. But they did comment that it was uncanny how the two of you appeared to be actually talking."

I ran a hand through my wet hair, debated spending time drying it, but coffee won out. Grabbing my bag, shoving my phone and charger into it, I slid my feet into my flip flops and headed for the door. "So I'm guessing Thor didn't want to come back here? He'd rather stay at your place? Alone?" I said over my shoulder as I left my apartment. Ben walked through the door to join me.

"It's his home. And he's used to spending time alone." He shrugged. "It's no big deal. But yeah, I'm sure he'll be looking for his breakfast right about now. And I had an idea."

"About?"

He cleared his throat. "I know you're going to need time to transition into eventually moving into my place. So I was trying to think of a way that would make it easier for you...like get you used to it in advance."

"Oh?"

"Just go to work every day. Use my house as your office, which it essentially is. So you're there every day, but when the work is done, you come back here. That way you'll be around for Thor and he can decide if he wants to come back here to sleep at night or stay at my place."

I thought about it for a minute. "You know that's not a stupid idea," I said, hurrying down the stairs. My blue Chrysler, circa 1970, sat at the curb. "I may have issues living in your house," I said, "but I have no such qualms about your car." Unlocking the driver's side door I climbed in, not even surprised when Ben was seated and waiting in the passenger seat. I was getting used to this. I never thought I would, yet here we were.

"Keys are in the bowl on the hallway table," Ben offered.

"What about your phone?" Pulling out from the curb, I took off with a roar, a backfire, and a cloud of smoke. I patted the dash in silent thanks. She'd done me well, but it was time for retirement.

"Dunno. I think the police took it."

Okay. I'd ask Galloway about it next time I saw

him. But then I could always just buy a new phone—
I had money now. Not even Ben's money, I had my
savings. Just over fifteen grand that was my deposit
for my own place...eventually. Like maybe when I
was around fifty. But all that had changed and here I
was, flush with cash. I had no idea how long the
process with Ben's estate would take, but until then,
I was okay.

"Where are you going?" Ben asked. "You missed
the turnoff."

"Firefly Bay Hotel," I replied.

"Errr. Why?"

"Coffee." For while my brain was functioning at a
marginal level sans caffeine, I knew it could do so
much better when I was fully caffeinated. And
grabbing a coffee at the hotel was killing two birds
with one stone.

"Okay...." Ben puzzled over my reasoning because
I hadn't yet explained to him my plan. It had been
bugging me since yesterday when we'd met with
Philip Drake. Aside from his odd behavior, he'd
called someone immediately after our meeting. And
I wanted to know who.

At the hotel, I managed to snag a table near a
power point and plugged my phone in.

"So what's the plan?" Ben asked from across the

table. It was weird because the chair was pushed in, so for him to sit on it he was effectively in the middle of the table.

"I need to get into Drake's office," I said, keeping my voice low. "And that's where you come in. I want you to go see if the coast is clear. Let me know when he leaves his office. If you could get a look at his appointments for the day that'd be even better."

Spying a waitress approaching, I stopped speaking and turned my attention to the menu.

"Good morning, ma'am." She smiled.

"Morning." I smiled back. "I'll have a long black please, and the eggs Benedict." I preempted her next question.

"Very well. Will that be all?" Before I could answer there was a loud rumble and a van pulled up outside the main doors. The waitress and I both turned to look.

"Oh no," she muttered, "that idiot. He's supposed to go around the back to the trade's entrance." I glanced at the van, saw the florist logo on the side, figured he was delivering a new bouquet for the reception desk until I saw the driver fling open the back doors and heave a giant urn out, with a floral display that had to be over five feet tall.

Brett Baxter appeared, rushing across the foyer,

clipboard in hand. "No, no, no." He wagged a finger at the driver. "You can't bring those through the foyer. We have guests."

"I got told to deliver 'em here and that's what I'm doing. You think you're the only place in town having a wedding today? I've got places I need to be. This is your delivery. I'll happily leave it here on the curb if you're going to give me grief." Wow. I admired the guy's bravado. Seemed Brett did too. I got the feeling that not very many people argued with him, so when they did, it got his attention. He eyeballed the driver who was an overweight man in his fifties, balding head, sweating profusely. The man rested the urn on the back of the van and eyeballed Brett. "Well? What's it going to be?"

"Very well. Just this once, mind you. In the future, kindly remember that all deliveries are to go to the rear of the hotel."

"I'm sure your guests won't mind looking at pretty flowers being delivered," he shot back.

"Breakfast won't be long," the waitress said, startling me.

I'd been so busy watching the driver and Brett that I'd forgotten she was there. I gave her a nod but kept my attention on the duo outside. Brett hijacked a luggage trolley but left all the heavy lifting to the driver, then led the way across the foyer while the driver pushed the flower-laden trolley. The driver was right. The flowers were really pretty. Brett appeared to be in his element, talking into a headset as he walked, referring to his clipboard, which on closer inspection was actually an iPad, before he and the driver disappeared from view.

"Nice day for a wedding," Ben commented, gazing out the window at the clear blue sky.

I shrugged. "Sure." Weddings stressed me out. I'd been a bridesmaid at my brother's and my sister's weddings and the pressure not to trip or knock anything over was amplified a million fold.

"I always thought I'd have a garden wedding," Ben continued, voice dreamy.

"Really?" I was shocked. "You thought about getting married?"

He shrugged. "One day, sure. When I found the right girl."

"I thought Tiffany may have been a contender." She'd been his latest. They'd been together six months before the whole thing had gone south. Six months was long-term for Ben. And he had the nerve to judge me on the brevity of my relationships.

"Nah. She didn't want kids."

I blinked. "I didn't know that."

His mouth turned down at the corners. "Doesn't matter now anyway."

We lapsed into silence when my coffee arrived. Moving my hand aside I accidentally brushed the cutlery in front of me onto the floor.

"I'm so sorry!" Appalled, I leaned over in my chair to scoop up the errant cutlery at the same time the waitress did, and we clashed heads. I jerked upright, slamming my head into the side of the table. "Owwww." Cradling my poor beat up head, I managed to right my cup of coffee before it tipped over and apologized, again, to the waitress. Her smile didn't reach her eyes. "I'll get you fresh cutlery." She spun on her heel and stalked away.

Careful not to burn myself, I took a grateful sip, while thinking about what Ben had said. "So...you wanted kids then?" It wasn't a topic Ben and I had talked about before.

"Of course. Don't you?"

"Well, yeah." Of course I did. Every time I was near my nieces and nephew my ovaries were fit to explode. My biological clock was well and truly ticking. "You'd have made a great father." It totally sucked that now we'd never know, he'd never get the opportunity.

"Don't go feeling sorry for me, Fitz," Ben warned,

wagging his finger in my face. I automatically made a snatch for it, forgetting he was a ghost until I felt the icy chill as my hand passed through his. I glanced around, hoping no one had seen me madly waving my hand around at nothing, and also feeling sad that I couldn't touch him anymore. It's the little things that get to you.

"Okay, I can see you're getting maudlin. I'm going to case the joint. Enjoy your breakfast." He disappeared as the waitress approached carrying a plate of food and replacement cutlery.

"Wow, that was quick."

"Saturday mornings are always busy for us." She slid the plate in front of me. "Can I get you anything else?"

"Nope, I'm all good, thanks." My stomach had begun rumbling as soon as it caught a whiff of the eggs Benedict. I waited until she'd turned away before picking up my knife and fork and tucking in. Oh so good. Hangover me liked the idea of going out for breakfast after a big night. I decided I'd make it a regular thing. But then once sober brain caught up I began thinking of Ben's case and why I was here. I was convinced the Armstrong case, the Drake case, and the Baxter case were all connected. The common denominator was the Firefly Bay Hotel.

But that's where my thought process stopped. All I had to go on was gut instinct that Philip Drake was up to something—I just needed to get a look at his phone and figure out who he'd called when I left his office yesterday. Easy, right?

17

*B*en returned and said the coast was clear. I finished breakfast, bolted down my coffee, paid and then made my way to Philip Drake's office, walking with confidence as if I had every right to be wandering the back corridors of the hotel. Of course what I was doing was a huge gamble. I was simply hoping that Drake wouldn't be in his office but his cell phone would be, which, when I thought about it, was madness. What type of hotel manager would he be if he didn't take his cell phone with him? But I remembered, when I met with him yesterday that he'd ushered me into his office and his phone had been on the desk. Most people would automatically pick it up and take it with them wherever they went.

As luck would have it, when I cracked open Drake's door and stuck my head in, I spied his cell phone sitting in exactly the same spot as yesterday. Slipping inside, I quietly closed the door behind me and darted behind his desk. My heart was thumping double time in my chest, adrenaline spiking.

"Keep a lookout," I told Ben, picking up the phone and swiping my hand across the screen. Damn it. Locked. "Use your torch app," Ben said. "Angle it toward his screen. You should be able to make out fingerprints on what buttons he pushes the most."

I gasped. "Is that how you crack a pin code?"

"Sometimes. It would be easier if we had an encryption app on your phone and synced it with his and blah, blah, blah," is what I heard. Ben was using a language I did not speak. Geek. Tuning him out, I did as he suggested and sure enough I could just make out what number he pressed the most. Not numbers, as in plural. Number, as in singular. The number three. Surely his pin wasn't three, three, three, three? It was! I almost squealed when I punched it in and the phone opened. Ben stopped yapping on about whatever it was and peered over my shoulder. "You did it! Well done!"

I couldn't believe it had been that easy. Pulling up

his phone log, I began scrolling. "What time were we in here yesterday?" I asked Ben.

"We were at the lawyers at two. That took about an hour, so maybe between three and three thirty?"

"Okay. At three twenty-two he called Sophie." There were no other calls around that time, in or out.

"Sophie's his daughter."

We looked at each other, puzzled. Drake had hired Ben to investigate Sophie's boyfriend. We assumed she didn't know about it, but what if she did? Because why else would Philip call her after my visit?

Two things happened next. One, I realized Ben was not keeping a lookout and two, Drake's phone started to ring. It startled me so bad I tossed it in the air, made a mad scramble to catch it, had just closed my fingers around it when I heard voices outside the door.

"Shit!" I whispered. Ben moved fast, crossing the room and poking his head through the door while I stabbed at the screen to get out of the call log. Pressing the button on the side of the phone, I rejected the call and sent it into sleep mode, then carefully aligned it back on the desk where I'd found it.

"Hide," Ben yelled. "He's coming."

"Where?" I whispered, frantically searching for a hiding spot. I eyeballed the desk. I could hide under it, but if he were to sit down he'd find me straightaway. Behind the curtains was a no go, they were sheer. I wouldn't fit in the filing cabinet, and believe me, I considered that option for a nanosecond, and unless the bookcase hid a secret door behind it, I was screwed.

Hurrying around his desk I eyeballed the sofa pushed back against the far wall. Fake it and pretend I was here searching for something I'd left behind yesterday? But I hadn't been anywhere near the sofa. I'd sat in one of the chairs opposite Drake's desk. The door handle began to turn and I darted toward the door, pressing myself up against the wall behind it, closed my eyes, and prayed.

"Ah, there it is." Philip Drake pushed the door open, it stopped an inch from my nose. I sucked in a breath and held it, praying he didn't shut the door and reveal my hiding spot. I heard his footsteps as he crossed the room and almost sagged with relief. So far, so good.

"As I was saying..." A male voice I didn't recognize spoke right next to me, making me jump.

"I think we can swing both the Roberts wedding on the seventeenth and the petit four cooking class."

"Baxter's the event manager. What does he say?" Philip Drake replied.

"He only cares about the Roberts wedding." The man sniffed. "He has no interest in what I do."

"The two of you have to work together," Drake grumbled, his footsteps returning. "It's imperative front of house and event management work together, not continually bring your squabbles to me."

Then the door closed and I listened as their voices faded away. Slumping against the wall, I exhaled the breath I'd been holding in a whoosh. A glance towards Drake's desk told me he'd returned to collect his phone.

"You are one lucky son of a b—" Ben drawled.

"You are one lousy lookout," I shot back. Gathering myself, I waited a few minutes for the coast to be clear, then quickly exited Drake's office. That had been a close call. Too close. My heart rate didn't return to normal until I was back in my car.

"Next time we do that," I huffed, "do a girl a solid and actually keep a lookout, will you?"

Ben had the grace to look contrite. "Sorry. My

bad. Too caught up in doing the investigative work, I guess."

"Okay then." I nodded. Fair enough. Ben wasn't used to being the lookout. He was used to doing the work. A lesson learned for both of us. I was just glad I hadn't been busted. "So what do you think?" I asked as I pulled away.

"About what?"

"The whole Sophie thing." I drummed my thumb on the steering wheel. "Did she know her dad had her boyfriend investigated? Was it just a coincidence that he called her after our visit yesterday?"

"On this occasion, despite me not believing in coincidences, it is possible."

"I think I should talk to Sophie," I decided.

"Risky."

"Risky is my middle name."

"No, it's not. Your middle name is—"

"If you say it I'll never speak to you again!" I shot him a glare. His answering smile was broad. "What do you know about Sophie?" I asked, distracting him.

"If I could remember I'd tell you."

Damn it, I'd forgotten. Post-death amnesia. How inconvenient. Gripping the steering wheel, I headed to Ben's house, or as he suggested I think of it—the office. I left my car on the street and smiled broadly when Mrs. Hill's curtains twitched. I waved and they quickly dropped back into place and I could see her in my mind's eye, hurriedly stepping back from the window as if I hadn't seen her spying on me in the first place.

"Where have you been? I'm starving!" Thor greeted me at the door and a pang of guilt had me scooping him up into my arms for a cuddle. "I'm sorry. I—" I was going to say forgot but bit off the words before they left my mouth. I didn't want him to know I'd forgotten him. Also, what was I thinking cuddling this cat? I was about to put him down when he head bumped my chin. I froze. Was he about to attack my face?

"Awww, look at you two," Ben purred. "That's nice."

"Nice?" I squeaked, still frozen with an overweight cream puff with delusions of badness cradled in my arms. But the purring emanating from Thor told me he didn't dislike me quite as much as he let on. Either that or he was just incredibly thankful I'd arrived to save him from imminent starvation.

"Come on, let's get you fed. And I really should get you some new bowls, huh?" I carried the ball of fur through the house, setting him down in the kitchen while I went to collect the kibble from the pantry.

"Thank you, human." Thor wound his way between my ankles and I had flashes of falling flat on my face, but the Gods must have been smiling on me for I kept my balance, poured the kibble into Thor's cereal bowl and returned the kibble to the pantry, all without incident. And then we had the coffee maker. The machine from hell. One coffee at the hotel had got me started. I'd need more if I was going to function further.

"Can you show me how to use this?" I jerked my head at the machine with all it's gleaming dials and buttons and longed wistfully for my ever so simple Keurig.

"Sure."

Ben's machine was the type where you add beans, press a button and the machine grinds the beans and makes your coffee. There was a steamer and frother and over a dozen variations of coffee I could make. I stuck with my very simple, very easy, long black. It was either master this machine or buy instant and I refused to buy instant. I wasn't a heathen.

Coffee made, I carried it into Ben's office and seated myself at the desk.

"Right, Sophie Drake. Who are you?" Shaking the mouse to wake up the computer, I opened the browser and then paused. "Do I need to erase your browsing history?" I said cautiously, a terrible thought occurring to me.

Ben snorted. "No. Why?"

"Oh, no reason." I gave a little hair toss and typed in Facebook. Best place to stalk a young woman? Social media. "Just want to make sure I'm not going to stumble across anything you wouldn't want me to see."

"Errr. Nope. I'm good." Then two seconds later. "Ooooh! You mean porn!"

Shaking my head, I blew out a breath. "Yes. Porn. Hence my question. Do I need to clear your browsing history because I don't want anything accidentally popping up."

"Popping up!" Ben hooted with laughter.

"You are so juvenile." Ignoring him, I began my search for Sophie. There were half a dozen Sophie Drakes with profiles on Facebook, but only one lived in Firefly Bay. I clicked it.

Ben got himself under control and muttered, "There's no porn. You're safe."

"Thank the Lord for small mercies." I was reading Sophie's profile. She was twenty, not the young teenager I'd thought, but a whisker off from being a fully-fledged adult. She was also a university student but didn't live at home, she lived on campus. Interesting. I wondered if that was to get away from a controlling father? Having your daughter's boyfriend investigated is pretty out there. Most of Sophie's posts were public and I made a mental note to talk to her about cyberstalking and protecting herself online. Then I fell into the rabbit hole of flicking through all of her photos. Over an hour had passed when a knock at the front door jolted me out of my voyeuristic activities. Sophie was a very attractive blonde and led a very active social life.

Having kicked my flip flops off, I padded barefoot to the door and flung it open, heard Ben mutter behind me about safety and checking to see who it is first.

"Oh hey." I greeted Detective Galloway. "I wasn't expecting to see you again so soon."

He flashed a smile. "Thought I'd drop by and sign those papers."

"Papers?" Oh shoot. The PI school stuff. With my family arriving last night—and subsequent bottle of red wine—it had totally slipped my mind. I chewed my lip, guilt written all over my face.

"You forgot, huh?" He rested a forearm against

the door jam in a pose that was straight out of a romance novel.

"Sorry." I ducked my head a little and shot him a look from beneath my lashes. "Come in though. We can do it now? If you've got time to hang around?"

I stood back a little and indicated he could come in if he wanted to. He did. He shot me another smile as he passed and my nose lifted to sniff the air in his wake, the scent of his cologne doing funny things to my insides. My eyes practically rolled into the back of my head. Mmmm. So nice.

"Fitzgerald. Head out of your pants," Ben whispered in my ear and I snapped to attention. Busted.

I followed Galloway, eyes glued to his denim-clad rear and berated myself the entire time for objectifying him this way. But man, he was put together just right and I couldn't help myself. He was a mixture of cowboy and cop—and while the cop part was a mood killer, the cowboy part more than made up for it.

"You got it all done then." Galloway stood in the living area with hands on hips while he surveyed the now tidy room around him.

"Yeah, sorry. It was a bit of a late-night with my family," I said.

"No need to apologize. You've got a lot going on, I get it. But I admit, I am here for another reason as well."

My heart picked up speed and my stomach did a little somersault in anticipation. He was going to ask me out. I knew it. I had to bite my tongue from blurting out yes before he'd actually asked the question.

"I was going through Ben's spreadsheet, and there were some links to some scanned documents that didn't get copied over to the USB. Could I get a copy of those too?" he asked. I knew my mouth dropped open. I felt it. Behind Galloway's left shoulder I saw Ben laughing, and my face heated in embarrassment. I wanted the floor to open and swallow me whole.

"Sure," I croaked, snapping my mouth shut. At least Galloway was oblivious to what was going on, well, sort of.

He frowned at me and cocked his head to one side. "Everything okay?"

"Yep. Yep." I nodded. He did not know I had the hots for him and I decided it was best to keep it that way, no matter what my ovaries were currently screaming to my brain. We had to work together. He was about to become my supervisor. Mixing work with pleasure was never a good idea. With that little pep talk out of the way I straightened my shoulders and shot him a dazzling smile. "Coffee?" I didn't wait for an answer. Instead, I swiveled on my heel and headed to the office to retrieve my cup. "I'm set up in here," I said over my shoulder.

Galloway followed. I left him peering at the monitor and photos of Sophie Drake while I made coffee. I jerked my head at Ben to follow me. Over the noise of the coffee machine I whisper shouted, "I need you to either make yourself scarce or not distract me when I'm working with Galloway."

"Oh, is working what we're calling it these days?" Ben teased. I slapped him on the arm, only of course he wasn't solid, so instead my hand sailed right through him and smacked into the side of the cupboard.

"Ow." Rubbing my wrist and the angry red mark, I glared at him. "You know what I mean. If I don't want to find myself in a mental institute I need to stay focused around him. He's trained to see things others don't. You don't think he's going to notice things like this?" I was madly pointing from myself to Ben and back again.

"Okay, okay, don't have an aneurysm. I promise I'll stay in the background and won't utter a sound."

I eyeballed him for another minute. Between a

talking cat and Ben's ghost it was going to be a
gargantuan effort not to let anything slip in front of
Galloway. We're not mentioning my hormonal
response to Captain Cowboy Hot Pants either.
Nope. We're pushing that down into a teeny tiny
little box, closing the lid and throwing away the key.

18

"*I* wouldn't have pegged her as your type," Galloway drawled when I returned to the office carrying two coffees.

Confused, I handed him his coffee. He was studying the monitor and the pictures of Sophie. "Oh!" the penny dropped. "She's not. It's one of Ben's cases. Actually, not her, her dad." I wondered if I should tell Galloway what I was working on. I mean, if he was going to be my supervisor I'd have to share information anyway, but it was going to take some getting used to...cooperating with the police.

It was like he could see the cogs turning in my head, knew the thought processes that were bouncing around like a very bad game of beer pong.

"I'll make this easy for you." He cradled his cup in

both hands and looked at me solemnly. "I can see you're having doubts. About trusting me. And I get it, I know what happened to Ben. I know he was treated unfairly and if I'd been around when he was still on the force, believe me, it would never have happened."

"That's easy enough to say. In hindsight," I pointed out.

He inclined his head. "Fair point. But you know I'm working toward fixing that. So be honest with me. What has you so reluctant to tell me what you're working on?"

"I'm worried you're going to take it for yourself. Take credit for it. Snatch it all up and say it's evidence in Ben's death and leave me with nothing." The words came out in a rush, running together so fast that even I had trouble understanding them.

But Galloway got the gist of it. He placed his cup on the desk, held one hand over his heart and the other up, palm facing me, and said, "I honestly swear that I will not take credit for any work Ben or you have done and that I will not steal his cases."

I smiled weakly. Now I felt like a knob.

"It's fine, Fitz," Ben said from the doorway. "Tell him everything. I'll vouch for him." I glanced Ben's way. If Ben trusted him that should have been enough for me and I wondered why it wasn't? Was it because I have such an overwhelming emotional response whenever he's around that it clouds my judgment?

"Fine." I huffed, pulling out the chair and sitting down. Galloway snagged the wooden chair from the corner again and dragged it over to the desk, making himself comfortable next to me.

Minimizing the browser, I pulled up the Delaney Investigations database and went through the open cases, giving Galloway a rundown on where I was at with each of them, finishing with this morning's activities.

Galloway looked at me with one brow raised. "You broke into his office?"

I shook my head. "No. It wasn't locked. So no breaking."

He sighed and shook his head. "Okay. No more of that. Let's keep you on the right side of the law, shall we?"

Whatever. "The point is, he called his daughter—who he was having investigated, well sort of—immediately after my visit. I was curious as to why."

Galloway pointed out the obvious. "Could be that he had plans with his daughter? Could be anything, not necessarily related to your visit at all."

"Maybe. Still. I think there's something there." I dug my heels in. Ben told me to trust my gut and my gut told me there was more to the Drake family. Philip Drake had been quick to pay me off, to close the job.

"Go back to Sophie's social media page," Galloway instructed. I pulled up the web page. "Pull up her photos, the ones other people have taken of her." I did as instructed. "What do you see?" I looked at the screen, at the grid of smaller images, all with Sophie in them, but there was one where her back was to the camera that looked vaguely familiar.

Then the penny dropped. "Holy shit!" I jumped to my feet in excitement, only my foot got tangled around the leg of my chair and before I knew it I was flat on my back staring up at the ceiling.

"You okay?" Galloway asked, his face a mixture of surprise and mirth.

"Yep." I clambered back to my feet and righted my chair before resuming my seat. Carrying on as if nothing had happened, I pulled up Ben's surveillance photos of Steven Armstrong and compared them with the photo of Sophie. Same hair, same build. "Could it be her?" I was talking to myself but Galloway answered.

"A strong possibility. So what should your next course of action be?"

"Talk to Sophie."

"Why not Armstrong?"

"Because he's older and is already used to lying to his wife. He'd have a cover story in place. I'm more likely to get the truth out of Sophie. Especially if I show her these photos."

"How so? What difference would that make?"

"Uh, hello? A twenty-something young woman on social media? Obsessed with her own image? She's going to want those photos."

Galloway smiled. "Good answer."

I sagged in relief, feeling like I'd passed a secret test. Okay, not so secret test.

"What about this next case? The Baxter one. What are your next steps?"

"Go through the journals he gave me, see if I can find anything remotely useful. Although I really don't know why Ben accepted this case. It's got me puzzled."

"This is the witch one, yes?" Galloway leaned over me to click the mouse. The Baxter file appeared on the screen.

"Yeah. I was curious because, one way or another, all three of these cases appeared to be linked to the

Firefly Bay Hotel. I wondered if that was why Ben took it on?"

"Really?" Galloway flicked through the files on the screen, scanning the information—information I'd already told him. Eventually, he sat back. "You're right. But again, it could be purely coincidental."

There's that word again. When, in the PI business, did you put something down to being truly coincidental and when do you call it pure bull hockey?

"I'm happy for you to pursue those lines of investigation." Galloway nodded.

I admit, it ruffled my feathers, having to get his permission. This was going to be a long twelve hundred hours.

"Thanks." I tried to keep my sarcasm to a minimum, but the snark was strong and he didn't miss it.

"You wanna back out?" he asked.

I shook my head. No, I did not. Without a word I pulled up the link to the PI school and began to fill out the online application. He watched in silence, then leaned forward, reading the screen.

"Your middle name is — ?"

"Don't you even!" I cut him off with a glare. "That name is never to be spoken. If we are going to have a successful working relationship we need to be very clear on this."

He jerked back in surprise, but a smile curled the edges of his mouth and that dimple flashed at me. Damn him. "Got it."

I finished filling it out and hit print. Galloway signed it. All that was left to do was mail it in and then wait to be formally admitted to PI School.

After I found the extra files he needed, I copied them on to a second USB and handed it over.

"Thanks." He took it from me and slid it in his pocket.

"Now what?" I asked.

"Now I go take down these corrupt bastards and you go interview Sophie Drake and read Baxter's journals," he drawled.

I frowned. "I know that." I huffed. "I meant...with us. How does this work?"

"Just call me when you need me. And don't do anything stupid. Or illegal," he added.

I followed him out of the office and to the front door. He left without saying goodbye and I watched from the front door as he crossed the lawn to his car. It was never going to be a hardship watching this man walk away. I sighed. Ben, who stood by my side, gave me an icy blast in the side, which I translated to be an elbow to the ribs.

"Yeah, yeah, I know," I whispered out the corner of my mouth. "Stop drooling."

Ben chuckled. "It's going to work out, Fitz. You'll see. You're going to ace PI school."

"I am?"

"How can you not? You've got Kade as your official supervisor, and then you've got me, who'll be working by your side every step of the way."

He had a point. "That almost feels like cheating."

"An advantage for sure," Ben agreed, "but you'll learn in this business to use everything and anything at your disposal to get the job done. And you have me. You can't fail."

"Oh God, don't say that! Murphy's Law kicks in whenever you say something like that," I protested.

A car door slammed and I turned my attention back to Galloway who gave me a wave before pulling away. I saw Mrs. Hill's curtains twitch again and frowned.

"What?" Ben asked, following my line of sight. "Problem?"

"No. Mrs. Hill is a busy body, for sure. I'm thinking if she's constantly got her nose glued to that window, then who better to ask about your visitors in the days leading up to your murder?"

Ben shrugged. "The police will have that under control. They've already got her statement."

He was right. And I was in no rush to go and speak with Mrs. Hill. It was doubtful she'd tell me anything, anyway, since I was her least favorite person on earth. Sighing, I returned inside, grabbed my bag and keys and it wasn't until I was pulling away in my 1970s Chrysler that I realized I'd forgotten to take Ben's car. Again.

"Sophie Drake?" I approached the blonde woman who was currently posing with duck lips taking selfie after selfie.

"Yeah?" She didn't even glance my way. Instead, she flipped through the images on her phone and bit out a sigh of frustration. "I'm off my selfie game today."

"Sorry to hear that." I wasn't, but then, she wasn't listening to me anyway.

"It's an assignment," she explained without looking up. "Social Media. I'm doing an essay on how to be an influencer."

"Right." Another minute passed. Then two. Okay, enough was enough. "Sorry to interrupt." I wasn't. "I'm Audrey Fitzgerald from Delaney Investigations. I was hoping I could ask you a couple of questions. It won't take long."

Her head jerked up and her blue eyes studied me, taking in my worn jeans, faded T-shirt, and flip-flops. The look on her face said she didn't approve of my fashion choices. "Who from who?" she asked.

"Audrey Fitzgerald," I repeated. "Delaney Investigations."

"What's that? Like, a health service or something?" She frowned.

I barked out a laugh, then realized she was serious. "Errr. No. It's a private investigator firm."

"Investigating what?"

"All sorts of things."

"Such as?"

"Background checks, missing persons, cheating spouses, lost pets." I rattled off cases I knew Ben had worked on in the past, watching her for any reaction. She blinked, her thick lashes brushing her cheeks. They were long and luscious and I wondered if they were fake.

"Oh." A light bulb went off. "Like a detective. I get it now." She smiled brightly, then turned her attention back to her phone. So. No reaction to me or my occupation.

"I have a rather delicate question to ask you."

She glanced up. "Oh?"

"Are you aware that Steven Armstrong is married?" Not exactly betraying a client's confidence, but I was skirting the boundaries. Ben had drummed it into me that I couldn't tell her about her dad hiring him to investigate her boyfriend. Or that Steven's wife hired him to prove he was having an affair.

Her lips flattened into a straight line and her eyes narrowed as she looked me up and down again. "Yeah well, that doesn't matter. We're in love." She sniffed. "He's leaving that deadbeat wife of his."

"Does your dad know?"

"Ha." She snorted. "He thinks I'm going out with that doped out of his skull loser, Logan Crane."

"You're not? Going out with Logan?" My gaze darted to Ben, who was peering over Sophie's shoulder, trying to get a look at her phone.

"As if. I just said that to get up Dad's nose. Looks like it worked." She eyeballed me again, then shivered, rubbed her arm where Ben had brushed against her.

He stepped back. "Nothing on her phone except pictures of herself," he told me.

"I'm guessing Dad hired you to get dirt on Logan and instead you caught me with Steven?" she asked, not at all surprised that her dad would do such a thing.

"Has he done that before? Hired a PI?" I asked, curious about the relationship between father and daughter. What had he said? That she'd been lying? Sneaking out? But she lived on campus, she didn't need to sneak out, she could come and go as she pleased.

She startled me by laughing, an honest to God belly laugh. I waited while she got herself under control. "Dad has had someone spying on me my entire life!" she declared. "Why do you think I'm living here? I knew it wouldn't stop him, but I figured giving him Logan would throw him off the scent and give me some peace for a while."

I glanced at Ben. As far as I knew this was the first time he'd done a job for Philip Drake. "It must be...annoying...having your dad do that." Annoying enough to kill the PI your dad had hired?

She shrugged. "Sure. Sometimes. To be honest, I thought it had stopped. The guy Dad had been using eventually refused to take on any more jobs. I don't know, maybe he got a guilty conscience? Or maybe it had something to do with me filing a stalking complaint?" She shrugged, but the look that she shot me was sly. She may like to look like a blonde airhead, but something told me Sophie Drake had plenty of street smarts.

"Interesting." I pulled out my phone and made myself a note to find out who that investigator had been. As far as I was aware, Ben was the only PI in Firefly Bay, but a city the size of Portland probably had a dozen PI's, if not more.

"What?" Sophie frowned and then peered at my phone, as if she could read what I was writing through the cracked screen. I held it against my chest, just in case. She seemed agitated now and that had me curious.

"I'm investigating the murder of my friend. Private Investigator Ben Delaney."

The color drained from her face, leaving her a pasty white. "What? I didn't kill anyone!"

My eyebrows rose. "I didn't say you had," I pointed out calmly. "But from what you just told me you're not above taking things into your own hands if you discovered your dad had hired another PI."

"I didn't know if he had or not," she blustered, the

color returning to her cheeks in a rush of pink. "But I assumed he would—at some point."

"Hence the lie about Logan. Give your dad something to chew on while you carried on an affair with a married man." My words were intentionally blunt. I didn't condone this young woman's actions in the slightest. "Quite the age gap too," I continued. "You know he's thirty-five? That's fifteen years older than you."

"I like older men." She sulked, crossing her arms across her chest.

"Let me give you some advice. When this all comes out—and it will—it's you who will come out of it worse off. You'll be labeled the other woman. The homewrecker. No matter that it's Steven doing the cheating. It's your reputation that will be dragged through the mud."

She gasped. "You can't tell anyone. That's against client privilege."

"I'm not a lawyer or a doctor," I pointed out, "so that doesn't apply, and also, your dad didn't hire Delaney Investigations to follow you. But you're right, I'm not telling anyone, that's not how I roll." I looked her up and down. "You seem a smart woman so let me give you one piece of advice, woman to woman. Once a cheater, always a cheater."

"Steven would never cheat on me!" she gasped.

I shook my head at her naivety. "Oh yeah? Whose bed does he sleep in every night? Who does he kiss good morning? He might tell you he doesn't love his wife or their marriage is dead or whatever way he spun it, but he's still there. With her. Because what he told you is bullshit just to get into your pants. And I'll bet you a hundred bucks he is most definitely having sex with his wife."

"Whoa!" Ben said, "Harsh."

"But true." I nodded my head emphatically. Which puzzled Sophie, because, of course, I was talking to a ghost. Damn it, and I had been doing so well. I cleared my throat and tried to cover the slip. "You're young, Sophie. You have your whole life ahead of you. There's plenty of time to find the right man. And a man who is married to someone else is not the right one. I think you know that, yeah? And maybe, on some level, you pursued this relationship to get back at your dad, but in the end, the one person you're hurting the most in all of this...is you."

19

*R*ather than park my ailing Chrysler on the street, I parked it in the garage next to Ben's Nissan. Maybe now I'd remember to take his car and let my old bucket of bolts enjoy her retirement.

Ben had grilled me all the way home about my speech to Sophie and how he thought I was talking from experience. I assured him I wasn't. I hadn't had an affair with a married man, and I hadn't been cheated on. But I'd had work friends who had. As a temp, I breezed in and out of people's lives, but believe me when I say I saw a lot of the fallout from those situations in the workplace. It was never pretty.

"Oh good—" Thor began when I opened the door leading from the garage to the house.

"Don't tell me." I cut him off. "You're starving?"

"Very good, human. You're learning." His British accent still slew me and I grinned as he trotted by my side on the way to the kitchen. As predicted, there was still kibble in his bowl. Rather than add more, I reached down and rearranged what was there, merely covering the empty spot in the center of the bowl. Thor didn't even notice. As far as he was concerned he had more food. I picked up the second cereal bowl that had an inch of water in it and took it to the sink for a clean and top up.

"You would have known when you took those photos of Steven kissing Sophie, who she was," I said to Ben while I worked.

He leaned against the kitchen bench, legs crossed at the ankles. "Yeah," he agreed.

"So I'm wondering if you didn't close the cases because of that connection? Sophie. In both cases, she wasn't the person you were hired to investigate, but there she was, right in the middle of both. I think you were planning on speaking with her—like I did today. Technically she hasn't done anything wrong. She's of legal age, she can see who she wants, but morally..."

Ben was nodding. "You're right. I was probably going to give her a lecture, in my cop voice, about the consequences of the choices we make."

"How much do you weigh? One eighty?" I measured him up out of the corner of my eye.

"Thereabouts." He shrugged.

"And Sophie? She's around five seven and a hundred and thirty-something pounds. Small frame."

"In that ballpark," he agreed. "And I see where you're going with this. She'd have struggled to get me into the woods. I'd have been dead weight."

"Did you notice though that the lawn isn't all dug up? There are no drag marks until you cross your boundary line and into the woods?"

He looked at me. "You're right." He eventually said, "I hadn't picked up on that." Before I knew it Ben was out the back door and on his hands and knees to examine the grass. Shaking my head, I placed the bowl of water down for Thor.

"Did you see who did it?" I asked the cat. It occurred to me that none of us had actually thought to ask the one other resident of the house if he'd seen anything.

Thor paused in his kibble-eating activities and sat back, tongue licking his snout. "I did not," he answered. "I was next door poking fun at the dog."

"It's you! You're the reason Percy barks so much, aren't you? You're winding him up!"

Thor yawned. "Can I help it that he has a pea-sized brain he doesn't use?"

"Thor, that's rude. And mean," I chastised, feeling sorry for Percy the pug. Now I felt bad for complaining to Mrs. Hill about her dog's barking when it was Thor to blame for riling him up in the first place. Thor just looked at me, then went back to eating, clearly not giving a toss.

"I need coffee," I muttered, making myself a cup while Ben crawled around the back lawn and Thor stuffed his face. I made a note to do some research on how much I should be feeding him because at the rate he was going he was going to be one overweight puss. Coffee in hand I finally faced what I'd been avoiding. Brett Baxter's journals. Stretching out on the sofa, the bag of journals on the floor, I pulled the first one out and began reading. I quickly realized one thing. They were incredibly boring. At first glance, in Brett's apartment, it had looked intriguing and I'd been slightly uncomfortable at the idea of Brett recording conversations and basically spying on the guests at the hotel. But now that I was actually reading one? What a yawn fest. A detailed record of each guest's fashion choices, complete with where he thought the items may have been purchased from, price range, and if he thought they were trashy or not. I started flipping through the pages, skimming over the fashion commentary before tossing the first journal aside. Only another eight to go.

It's entirely possible I dozed off, for the next thing I knew there was a banging coming from the front door and I had a book on my face. Struggling up, I dislodged the book, and Thor, who'd been curled up by my side. With sleepy eyes, he shot me an accusing glare before moving grudgingly to the end of the sofa where he resumed his nap.

The banging continued. Straightening my T-shirt, I glanced out the back windows. Ben was still intent on the lawn investigation, although he was over near the border of his property now, where the grass gave way to dirt.

Stumbling my way to the front door, I assumed it was Detective Galloway so threw open the door and barked, "What?"

Only it wasn't Galloway who was pounding with fist raised. It was Steven Armstrong. He barged inside, shouldering me out of the way. I staggered and reached out a hand to steady myself. "Hey! That was rude," I told him. Now that he was in the house he didn't know where to go, so he spun on his heel and glared at me, hands on hips. I could only assume he'd had a call from Sophie.

"You've been spying on me!" he accused.

"I"—I pointed to myself—"have not." Which was true. It wasn't me. But I was splitting hairs.

"You told Sophie you knew about our relationship."

"Now that part is true." I nodded. I wasn't scared of him although I could tell he wanted me to be. He was all bluster and anger and he thought by towering over me I'd be cowed. Clearly he hadn't met me. One sharp knee to the gonads would bring him down and if he came any closer he was going to discover that for himself.

"Why?" He almost cried the word, it was so beseeching.

"Oh, was it a secret?" I batted my eyelashes and flattened my palm to my chest, mocking him. "What's wrong? Don't want your wife to find out?"

"You bitch," he growled. I saw the fist coming. Rather than dodge away I stepped closer, raised an arm to block while simultaneously bringing my knee up into his groin. Hard. His punch deflected off my forearm but still hurt like the devil. His strange mewling noise was incredibly rewarding, made especially sweet when he looked at me, mouth open, eyes crossed. His hands clutched his family jewels and he ever so slowly toppled sideways, where he curled up into a ball on the entryway floor. Figuring he'd be incapacitated for a couple of minutes at least, I retrieved my phone from the living room and called Galloway.

"Audrey," he answered.

"If someone were to throw a punch at me, in my own home, and I kneed them in the nuts...is that assault?" I asked conversationally, walking back to keep an eye on Steven who was still curled in the fetal position.

"That would be self-defense on your part. Assault on the other party's part. This isn't a hypothetical, is it?" he asked, his voice resigned.

"Sadly, no."

"Are you in danger? Where is this person now?"

"On the floor. I think he might be crying?" I added, peering at the sniveling excuse for a man.

"On my way." He hung up and I was listening to the dial tone. I don't know what possessed me, but I snapped a photo. For my own personal collection, I told myself. I'd never post it on social media.

Although it would serve as a handy reminder to any male who thought it was okay to strike a woman. I leaned back against the wall and crossed my arms, waiting for Galloway to arrive. Every now and then Steven would move, then groan, then sniff. I cocked my head, watching him, and wondered if I'd busted a nut? I supposed it was possible, but so help me I didn't feel bad about it.

I heard the siren seconds before the screech of tires out front. Stepping over Steven, I crossed to the front door and opened it, watching as Galloway strode up the garden path. I made a mental note that he was just as easy to look at walking toward me as he was away.

Galloway ran his eyes over me as if assuring himself I was still in one piece, then looked beyond me to the man curled up inside. His face was stern, but I could tell he was trying not to smile.

"Okay. Tell me what happened," he said.

I did, telling him what had happened, what Steven had said before his misguided attempt to assault me.

Ben arrived, eyeballed Steven who had barely moved, then looked to me and Galloway. "What's happened?" His voice was shocked and I shot him a look, trying to convey that I could hardly answer him with Detective Galloway standing right in front of me.

Galloway was nodding. "That's a good move," he said when I described how I'd managed to get the jump on a two hundred-pound angry man.

I grinned. "Self-defense classes finally came in handy."

"And you're sure you're not hurt," he pressed. I lifted the arm that had blocked Steven's blow. The throbbing had stopped and a nice bruise was forming along my forearm. Galloway's face darkened when he saw the mark. Swiveling, he stepped inside and dragged Steven to his feet, who protested with a pained whine.

Galloway had zero sympathy. "Hands behind your back," he demanded. Steven reluctantly let go of his balls and did as instructed. "Steven Armstrong, you're under arrest for assault. You have the right to remain silent. Anything you say can and will be used against you in a court of law. You have the right to an attorney. If you cannot afford an attorney, one will be appointed for you."

He marched Steven out of the house, past me, toward his car, lights still flashing on the dash. I followed. After securing him in the back seat,

Galloway slammed the door and then came back to speak to me where I stood on the edge of the lawn.

"I don't want to press charges," I said.

"Too late. I've arrested him." Galloway shrugged. "Hold up your arm," he instructed. Puzzled, I did. Galloway snapped a photo of the bruise with his phone. "Evidence," he muttered. "And you're going to have to come in and give a statement."

"Can't you do that here?" I admit, my own voice came out whiny. Once upon a time, I used to love visiting Ben in his workplace. Not anymore. I had no desire to be sitting in an interview room knowing cameras were watching me, recording me, and being potentially used against me.

"You still need to be fingerprinted—relax, not as a suspect. We need them for Ben's case, so we can rule out your prints and Ben's and see what's left."

He was right. I was meant to do that and I'd been putting it off until I'd conveniently forgotten about it. I was surprised they hadn't been on my case before now. Reading my mind, Galloway grinned. "I was going to call you in on Monday. When Officer Jacobs is on. I don't want you having to deal with Mills." Meaning Officer Mills was working this weekend.

I inclined my head. "I appreciate that."

"So I'll see you Monday. Providing you can stay out of trouble that long." He touched his hand to his brow in salute and climbed into his car. I stood and watched until the SUV was out of sight, noticing Mrs. Hill's curtains twitch when I finally turned to go back inside.

20

"How did it go with the grass?" I asked Ben once I'd closed the front door.

"Don't think you can distract me that easily!" He floated along beside me, sitting in an armchair opposite when I slouched back onto the sofa. Thor was nowhere to be seen and I figured he'd scampered outside when Steven had started shouting.

"Look, I'm fine." I protested. While it was nice to be around men who cared, it could also get just a little smothering. "I dealt with it. He didn't take me by surprise, I could tell by his body language that he would probably attack at some point, and he did. Plus, I'd taken that self-defense class you recommended, remember?"

Ben didn't look happy about it and I knew it must be frustrating for him not to be able to protect me. "I assume he was here because of Sophie?" Ben said.

I nodded. "He dug his own grave there. He's terrified of his wife finding out, yet now word is bound to leak with him being arrested for assault. Also, I don't think he killed you."

"Oh? He's male. Roughly the same size and build as me. It could have been him Mrs. Hill saw through the window."

"He seemed genuinely distraught that someone had found out about his affair with Sophie. It was an instinctive reaction for him, to come forcing his way inside here and unleash his emotions on me. And while he did attempt to hit me, he didn't come with a weapon to kill me. If he's behind your murder, then a: he would already know that people know and he would have reacted differently. Angry? Yes. But not surprised. He'd have been more in control. And, b: he wouldn't have confronted me the way he did. If he'd wanted to silence me he'd have done better to wait until it was dark and then make his move. Like he did with you—if he was the killer."

"You have a point. You have a talent for reading people, Fitz."

I shrugged. "A skill you subconsciously pick up with temping. You get pretty good at summing people up. It can be brutal in the workforce, resentments and jealousy run rife." The temping life reminded me a lot of dating. You'd turn up to an assignment and it was like you were the only single girl at a party—all the other wives thought you were there to steal their husbands—only at work, they thought you were going to steal their jobs. Everyone was so darn insecure, it was sad when you thought about it.

"That bruise looks pretty bad." Ben motioned to my arm. The blow had landed on the underside of my forearm and still throbbed, despite that I'd told Galloway it didn't hurt. He'd have made me go to the hospital if I let on I was in pain, and I had no intentions of another emergency room visit over a simple bruise.

I peered at it. Ben was right though, the bruise was pretty nasty. The red was changing to purple and dark blue blotches were appearing. "I think I'll ice it." Grabbing a packet of peas out of the freezer, I held them to my arm.

Ben was trying to pick up one of Brett's journals but having no luck. "I don't know about those." I sank back down onto the sofa and nodded at the journals strewn across the coffee table. "They're boring. Mostly fashion commentary. I've not come across anything remotely resembling witchcraft. I'm starting to wonder if Brett doesn't have some sort of mental disorder?"

"I wonder why I took the case then?" Ben leaned forward, elbows on knees, head hung low as he examined the rug beneath his feet.

"Hey," I said in a soothing tone. "It's not your fault you can't remember. I'll keep at it." He lifted his head and looked at me. "How did it go outside?" I nodded toward the back garden. "You were examining the grass pretty intently."

He flopped back in his chair, mimicking my pose. "I dunno. With so many people traipsing to and from the crime scene, it's been totally flattened."

"I'm sorry." I could see how frustrating it was to follow a lead to a dead end. I'd only just started this new career and I was already thinking in terms of leads and clues and dead ends.

"You had to have known, when you took the photos of Steven, that the woman involved was Sophie Drake." I leaned my head back and gazed up at the ceiling.

"Yeah."

"What would you do? Like, now? Knowing what

we know, that it is Sophie Steven is having an affair with. What would your next steps be?"

"I'd go talk to them," he said. Which is exactly what I thought he'd do. "While it's technically none of my business what they do, it wouldn't hurt to give them a little shakeup that a PI is sniffing around, and to have some home truths how their actions are hurting others."

"That's what I thought," I murmured. "That's why you didn't close out the cases. You were tying up your own loose ends. And the Firefly Bay Hotel connection was coincidental after all." I was deflated over that particular fact. I'd felt so sure there was something going on at the hotel that involved all three of Ben's cases. Which reminded me. Pulling out my phone, I squinted at the photos I'd taken of Brett's wall, but the cracks in my screen didn't allow for easy viewing. Instead, I emailed them to Ben's business address, then headed into his office to view them on the monitor.

"These don't make any sense." I sighed. Brett had pinned his work rosters on the wall, highlighted a different staff member's name on each roster, then pinned a red string from it to a black silhouette of a woman in the middle. On the other side were random people's names scribbled on scraps of paper and given the same treatment. Everything led to the silhouette of the woman, but there was no clue who the woman was. "Maybe she's not a woman but a representation of something," I said out loud.

"It's very odd. And it's also puzzling that Brett didn't invite you to see this for yourself. If it's part of his research." Ben stood behind me, peering over my shoulder.

"The first journal Brett showed me had snippets of conversations he'd overheard while at work. Yet so far, the other journals don't have anything like that in them. Most of it is judging people's fashion choices and bitching about his colleagues."

"So something changed. Something triggered this latest obsession."

"Latest obsession? Why would you say that?" I craned my neck to look at him.

He blinked at me in surprise. "I don't know," he admitted.

I pounced. "You remembered something!"

"That Brett Baxter is obsessive is hardly a breakthrough," he drawled.

"But you said 'the latest obsession.' Meaning you knew he'd had previous obsessions. So you must have known something about him that isn't in his file."

"The question is what? And is it relevant?" He frowned at the computer screen. "And are we wasting our time here?"

I had a thunderbolt of a thought. "What if you turned Brett down, said you wouldn't take his case, and he lost it and killed you? I know he's not the same build as you, but he's male and probably strong enough to drag you into the woods."

Ben shrugged. "It could have been him, I suppose. But then whoever killed me may not be related to my cases at all," he pointed out.

"Yes, but whoever it was, you trusted enough to let them into your house. And you were in your kitchen when you were attacked. Maybe offering them a drink or something?"

"There's a lot of maybes."

He was right. I was guessing. The buzz of my phone interrupted us.

"Audrey Fitzgerald," I answered, not recognizing the number.

"Good afternoon, Audrey, this is the Firefly Bay Helping Hand Facility."

"Oh. Hi." The facility that cared for Ben's dad.

"I'm so sorry to hear about Bill Delaney's son, Ben," the woman continued, "We'd like to pass on our sincere condolences."

"Thank you."

"Also, we did receive word from McConnell's that you now have power of attorney of Bill's affairs?"

I nodded. "That's right."

"Okay, excellent. We've got everything we need from McConnell's, but we do need you to pop in at some stage and provide us with photographic I.D. Just for our records, you understand."

"That's fine, I can do that. I need to come in and visit with Bill anyway. Does he know? That Ben died?"

"He does not. It's highly doubtful he would understand or comprehend it."

"Oh. That's so sad." Alzheimer's was an awful disease. "So do you think I should tell him?" I chewed on my nail.

"Maybe when you come in talk to one of the doctors?" she replied. "They'd be a better judge of that."

I nodded. "Yeah, that sounds like a good idea. I'll do that. Actually..." I glanced at the time. "Could I come in now?" It was almost three thirty. I figured I could drop into the care facility on my way home.

"Of course. Just report to reception. We'll have everything waiting for you."

"Thank you." Disconnecting the call, I looked at Ben, who had moved over to the sliding door overlooking the back garden and was looking outside.

"You wanna come visit your dad with me?" I asked.

"Yeah. Just...prepare yourself, Fitz, okay? He won't know who you are. That can be confronting when it's someone you've known your whole life and they don't remember you."

I reached out to lay my hand on his shoulder, only of course my hand moved right through him and hit the window instead. "Shit."

Ben chuckled. "Another thing to get used to, eh?"

"Have you seen Thor? I want to let him know I'm leaving and see what he wants to do." Words I thought I'd never say. Checking in with a cat.

"Not since he shot out the cat door when Armstrong arrived."

Sliding the glass door open, I figured I should at least make an effort to find the feline. "Thor!" I called, stepping out onto the deck, hand raised to shield my eyes from the afternoon sun. I scanned the garden for movement. None. Not even a twitch of a fuzzy tail. I called his name again and stepped down onto the grass, scouted the entire back garden with no sign of the furry terror. "Come on, Thor!" I bellowed. Then I heard it. Percy barking.

"I bet you're next door stirring up the dog," I muttered, spinning on my heel and heading toward the gate that separated the two properties. Sure enough the gate was ajar, a big enough gap for one overweight puss to squeeze through. Pushing the gate open further, I stepped through. Mrs. Hill's back garden was beautiful. Laid out in a country cottage style, with a little hedge bordering a paved area with a birdbath in the center, garden beds full of shrubs in bloom, a yellow birch dominating one corner.

"Thor!" I whisper-shouted. I'd never been in Mrs. Hill's garden before and it didn't feel right being here, despite the fact that she quite frequently used the gate to cross onto Ben's property. Something told me if she knew I was in her back garden she wouldn't be happy. Percy was inside and his barking escalated when he heard me. Damn it, he was going to get me busted.

I darted across to the house and pressed my back against the wall, just in case Mrs. Hill peered out one of her back windows to check what the ruckus was about. But of Thor, there was no sighting. Maybe he wasn't here after all. Maybe he was in the woods and

I wasn't ready to go in there yet. I wasn't sure I'd ever be ready; just the thought of it had flashes of Ben's body appearing in my mind—a sight that could never be erased.

"Darn cat." I cursed, tiptoeing back to the gate and not breathing easy until I was back on the other side. I closed the gate, made sure the latch clicked. "If you're over there and ignoring me," I stage whispered again, "you're going to have to jump your lazy ass over the fence to get home." Still no reply and a tinge of worry had me chewing my lip again.

"He'll be fine," Ben said when I went back inside, minus one cat. "He's probably asleep in one of his favorite sunny spots."

"In the woods?" I asked, casting a dubious glance at the woods looming alongside Ben's garden.

"Affirmative."

"Fine." I huffed. "I'll go see your dad and then swing back past here to check on him, see if he wants to come back to my place." There was still plenty of water and kibble in his bowls so I knew he'd be okay, but my maternal pet instincts were kicking in and, okay, I admit, I was worried about leaving him alone in the woods. What if he got hurt? What if some bigger animal figured he was prey? I never cared before because Thor was Ben's cat—I saw him as a nuisance. Now he was wriggling his way into my heart and I didn't know what to think about that.

"Awww, look at you," Ben teased. "You're worried about him. Audrey Fitzgerald, you're turning into a cat person."

"Wash your mouth out," I grumbled, but I smiled, snatched Ben's keys from the bowl in the foyer and headed out.

*B*en was right. It was heartbreaking to see his dad. Dementia had really taken its toll. His short term memory was completely gone and his long term memory was now affected. Bill Delaney was a sixteen-year-old youth living in a sixty-year-old body.

"You're pretty," he told me as we sat drinking tea in the garden of the care facility.

"Thank you." I smiled.

"What's your name again?"

"Audrey. Audrey Fitzgerald. I'm a friend of your son's."

William spat his tea back into his cup with a snort of laughter. "That's hilarious." He giggled. "I don't have a kid. Gosh." He leaned forward to whisper to me, "I'm still a virgin. I haven't ever..."

My face heated at having such a conversation with Ben's dad—a man who'd been a second father to me. I took another sip of my tea. I was a coffee girl, but I could choke down tea when the occasion warranted it, and since Bill had insisted on tea because his dad said he was too young to be drinking coffee, we were drinking tea.

"See?" Ben whispered in my ear and I gave a slight nod to indicate I'd heard him. The care facility was nice enough, I suppose, although the locks on every door and gate were disconcerting. But dementia patients had a habit of escaping, so keeping them locked in was for their own safety. I understood that, but it still made me incredibly sad. I'd handed over my ID at the reception desk and had my photo taken so they could upload it to their system. I'd also met with one of the facility's doctors who'd advised me not to mention Ben's death to his dad. He was concerned it would only lead to more confusion and ultimately distress for Bill.

"So what do you want to be when you grow up, Bill?" I asked, trying to move the conversation away from his non-existent virginity.

"A mechanic!" Bill nodded with great enthusiasm,

then launched into a monologue on cars he'd like to work on and cars he'd like to own. I smiled and nodded where appropriate, all the while my heart aching.

And then he said something that jarred me alert. "Ben's neighbor had a Cadillac in really great condition, a collector's piece it was, till that nephew of hers got hold of it." I almost spilled my tea.

"Do you mean Mrs. Hill? Ethel Hill?" I asked, afraid to hope that he'd actually remembered anything.

"Ahhh, Ethel. Always was a looker." He sighed dreamily. "She's older than me by a few years, but that doesn't bother me. An older woman has more experience, you know." He winked.

"And Ben?" I prompted.

"Who's Ben?" He frowned and my heart sank. "Do you mean Brett? Her nephew?" he added.

"Brett?" It couldn't be...could it? The name Brett was pretty common but what if Brett Baxter was Ethel Hill's nephew? "Brett Baxter?" I asked.

"That's him. Looney tune that one." And then he was back into his world of cars, how the girl he liked, Beryl Sanderson, drove a VW Beetle and it was as cute as she was. I grinned. He'd ended up marrying Beryl Sanderson and it made my heart happy that he was at least remembering some of his life and the love that he had for a woman for decades.

I finished up my visit with Bill, then spent ten minutes searching for my car in the parking lot before remembering I was in Ben's Nissan. Ben had decided to visit with his dad a while longer, so I pulled out of the lot and headed back toward Ben's house, pondering how ghosts could travel while I enjoyed my new smooth ride. This thing felt like I was driving on marshmallows, and the steering! Oh my God, it was so light compared to my Chrysler. Not to mention the speakers, and the GPS, and the cruise control and integrated Bluetooth. Ben had critiqued my driving and basically stressed the entire drive to the facility, but now I was alone I got to enjoy the ride, and enjoy it I did, with the volume cranked and the windows down—did I mention they were power windows?—I was almost happy. Until I thought about the source of my happiness and then my mood quickly soured. I loved the car. What I didn't love was the fact that I only had it because my best friend had died. I was going to have to find a way to reconcile these emotions before they messed me up.

Instead I concentrated on what Bill had said,

about Ethel Hill and her nephew. Of course, it could have been the ramblings of a man suffering from dementia, but what if he had a brief moment of clarity? The doctor had told me that Alzheimer's is a common cause of dementia and brief moments of clarity could happen, only it wasn't a frequent occurrence and those flashes were simply that—flashes. He'd warned me that Bill's life expectancy would be cut short due to his illness. The average was six to ten years, and Bill had been living with this for more than three, possibly longer because it went undiagnosed for a period of time. Shaking away the maudlin thoughts, I connected my phone to the Bluetooth in the car and called Mom.

"Audrey, love, everything okay?" she answered on the second ring.

"All good, Mom. Hey, I have an odd question. Is Brett Baxter Ethel Hill's nephew?"

"Why, yes, he is."

Boom! I had my answer. I slapped the steering wheel. Now it made sense. Ben took Brett's case as a favor. It was a bullshit case, but I bet Mrs. Hill pressured him into it.

"Are you driving?" Mom intruded in my thoughts, reminding me she was still on the line.

"Yeah. I went to visit Mr. Delaney," I told her.

"How's he doing?" I filled Mom in on my visit with Ben's dad and we chatted until I arrived back at Ben's. Parking the car in the garage, I let myself into the house. While talking with Mom I'd come up with a sort of plan. I needed to get Mrs. Hill talking and the best way to do that was to get her to make the first move. If I knocked on her door and started asking questions she'd probably slam the door in my face. How to get her to make the first move? Annoy her.

Step one, reverse my oil leaking Chrysler onto the driveway and leave it there—on the pretense of accessing the gardening tools hanging on the rear wall of the garage. Step two, start gardening. I was reasonably confident that whatever I attempted to do gardening wise, Mrs. Hill would have an opinion on it. And it would be that I was doing it wrong. I was the first to admit I did not have a green thumb, and I didn't want to ruin Ben's beautiful garden, so I picked the simplest thing. Rake the lawn. Despite it not being fall and there were no leaves to rake, I set to with the rake, dragging it across the grass. Sure enough, the curtains twitched in the window next door and minutes later she was out the front door and crossing her front lawn. I bit back a smile.

"You should smile more, dear. You don't look like

you're enjoying gardening," she said.

"But I'm not." It wasn't entirely true. This was the first time I'd done anything in the garden since I'd lived at home almost ten years ago.

"And it shows, dear. And if you look like you're not enjoying it, well"—she glanced around then leaned in to faux whisper—"it makes it look like you can't afford a gardener."

I straightened, leaning on the rake. "But I can afford a gardener," I pointed out.

"That may well be the case dear, but this"—she waved a hand at me—"screams poverty." I stiffened at the thinly veiled insult. Yes, my jeans weren't designer label, and my T-shirt was from Target. So what? And how she collated me doing the gardening to mean I was poverty-stricken was beyond me.

"Actually I'm glad I got you." I smiled sweetly. "I was hoping to ask you about your nephew, Brett."

She blanched and clutched her pearls. "I have nothing to say about that boy." With that, she spun on her heel and disappeared into her house, no doubt to polish her silverware. Or pearls. Or whatever it was she did with her time when she wasn't busy spying on her neighbors.

I continued to rake the lawn, despite it being entirely unnecessary, while I pondered the riddle of

Brett Baxter. Given Mrs. Hill's reaction when I mentioned him, maybe she hadn't pressured Ben to take his case after all. I'd have to wait for Ben to return from visiting with his dad before I could discuss it with him. Not that he remembered the details, but simply talking it over out loud would give me some insight. Which reminded me. Had Thor turned up yet? I'd just returned the rake and was preparing to put my Chrysler in the garage when Mrs. Hill's front door opened and she stepped outside.

"Audrey, dear," she called with a little wave. I stopped on the driveway and watched as she hurried across the lawn. "I've considered what you said and I may possibly have been too hasty. Perhaps you'd like to come in for a cup of tea and I'll tell you what you want to know?" I blinked in shock. Mrs. Hill being nice and inviting me in for tea?

"Ummm. Okay, yes. Sure," I stuttered, totally thrown. Wiping my palms on the seat of my jeans, I followed her across to her front door.

"Take your shoes off, dear."

"My shoes?"

"Yes, dear. We don't want you leaving a scuff mark, do we? She looked pointedly at my feet and I sighed, toeing off my shoes to leave them on the doormat. She tsked dramatically, bent and lined them up with perfect precision. "You know I found the best way not to leave scuff marks is to only wear leather." I glanced at my ten-dollar canvas shoes. Definitely not leather.

"Tea?" She smiled sweetly and beckoned me to follow her to the kitchen. Her house was everything I'd expected. It smelt like lavender and beeswax. Doilies abounded, and vases with flowers adorned every room. A scrambling scratching noise on the floorboards heralded Percy's arrival. The rotund pug waggled his way down the hallway with great excitement, sniffing and snuffling around my ankles, licking the top of my foot and making me giggle.

"Hey there, Percy," I greeted him, ruffling the top of his head.

"Percival," Mrs. Hill corrected.

"Sure." I shrugged. I didn't mention that Percy's claws were probably scuffing her floors more than my shoes ever could have. I followed her into her kitchen. Her house had a vastly different layout to Ben's. Where his was an open plan with big comfy sofas and an overall casual style, hers was a cottage, with a very feminine vibe. Florals and lace was the theme throughout, and rather than open-plan she had a separate living room, dining room, and kitchen. Floral curtains hung from the window and the countertops were adorned with a collection of miniature figurines—mostly pugs. I stood awkwardly while she put a whistling tea kettle to boil on the stovetop and lifted down a royal blue teapot.

"Why don't you make yourself comfortable in the dining room, dear, rather than hovering over me, hmmm?"

I nodded and brushed past her. Her kitchen was galley style, with a door either end. The dining room was dominated by an oval table with a lace tablecloth and a huge vase of flowers in the center. The windows overlooked her back garden, although you couldn't see much due to the heavy lace curtain obscuring the view. Taking a seat, I fiddled with the tablecloth, wondering what had made her change her mind and invite me in for tea. It was so out of character for her. Although to be fair, I didn't really know her, just that when we first met she didn't seem to like or approve of me and we'd continued to butt heads ever since. Maybe because we were going to be neighbors she'd had a change of heart. And maybe I should take a leaf out of her book and make an effort.

"Sugar cookie?" she called from the kitchen. "I

baked them myself."

"Oh. Errr. Sure." Okay, this was weird. I felt like I was in an alternate universe. My toes curled against the rug on the floor and I glanced around, a sense of unease settling over me. I wished Ben were here to lend moral support. An old fashioned wind-up clock sat on the dark wood dresser pushed up against the wall, its ticking the only other sound aside from Mrs. Hill bustling around in the kitchen.

"You want to know about my nephew?" She appeared carrying a tray, two cups complete with saucers, and a small plate with scalloped edges that held an artful array of sugar cookies.

"If that's okay?" I felt like I was on the back foot and I watched her shrewdly, wondering if that had been her intention. For I was on her home turf now, she had the upper hand.

"It depends on what you want to know, dear."

I took a cookie and nibbled on it. "I've inherited Ben's business, along with his house, and he'd recently taken Brett on as a client," I explained.

She stiffened for a nanosecond before busying herself setting out the teacups. "Oh?"

"Well...Brett's case is somewhat...fanciful, I guess you could call it. I'm surprised Ben agreed to take him on as a client at all."

"Brett is a conspiracy theorist." She sniffed. She may as well have said drug dealer for all the disdain in her voice.

"Conspiracies? Such as?" Elbows on the table, I leaned forward.

"He thinks everyone who works at the hotel is Illuminati." She straightened the floral apron around her waist. I only just noticed she was wearing one, it blended that well with her dress.

"Illuminati? As in the secret group? The one that is supposedly set to create a new world order?"

She shrugged. "I really don't know who or what the Illuminati is, my dear, some sort of group, yes, I suppose so."

I frowned, picturing the pins on Brett's wall.

"He also believes that a UFO really did crash in Roswell in the forties and that the aliens on board—along with their spacecraft—are being held at Area 51." He wasn't alone in that theory, plenty of people thought that. The shrill whistle of the kettle boiling negated further conversation, but I heard Mrs. Hill say something about reptilians as she bustled back into the kitchen to finish making the tea. I chewed on the sugar cookie shaped like a Christmas tree as I digested what she'd told me.

22

The tea, when I took a sip, was incredibly bitter and I couldn't help my reaction. My face screwed up like I'd sucked a lemon.

"Sugar?" Mrs. Hill had taken a seat opposite me after pouring us both a cup from the blue teapot that now sat between us. She pushed a crystal sugar bowl closer to me.

"Sorry." I schooled my face. "It has quite an...unusual...flavor. What sort of tea is it?" I'm not a big tea drinker, but this was nothing like the tea I'd had at the care facility when I was visiting Ben's dad.

"It's an herbal blend I made myself. From the flowers in my garden." My gaze shot to the window and the garden outside. The bitterness lingered on my tongue and I hoped whatever she'd used in the tea hadn't been laced with weed killer. I stirred in a teaspoon of sugar, and then added another just to be safe. Mrs. Hill took a sip of her own tea, so I figured the weed killer theory wouldn't hold water.

"So has Brett always been a conspiracy theorist?" I picked up the conversation from where we'd left off.

"He's always had fanciful notions." She nodded her head ever so slightly, her eyes glued on me.

"Did you know he'd asked Ben to investigate one of his theories?" I choked down another mouthful, my eyes watering. I was doing my best not to be rude, but the tea was awful. I ran my tongue over my teeth which was when I realized my face kinda felt numb.

"I did not, no." This time a slight shaking of her head. I frowned down into my teacup. I'd gulped down half the contents when a terrible thought occurred to me. What if I were allergic to one of the ingredients? My lips were tingling, my face was numb, I was having some sort of reaction without a doubt. My heart skipped a beat. What if it spread? What if my throat closed over and I couldn't breathe? Okay, stay calm Audrey, just get yourself to hospital.

"Methers Hill?" I lisped, struggling to get the words out, "Coll bulnce."

She cocked her head. "What's that, dear? You'll have to speak more clearly. That's the problem with people today, they don't enunciate."

I stood so fast my chair tipped over, crashing to the floor, while I clutched my throat, panic sweeping through me. "Help," I croaked.

Mrs. Hill stood, stacked the cups back onto the tray and carried them back into the kitchen while I stood aghast, gasping for breath. The edges of my vision were starting to blur and finally my confused brain caught up. The tea had been poisoned. I'd been joking about the weed killer, but it seemed I had misjudged Mrs. Hill entirely. Spinning on my heel, I ran for the back door, the closest exit, only my legs wouldn't obey. What should have been a sprint was more of a shuffle. But still, I gave it a red hot go, staggering toward the door, using the walls to keep myself upright, knocking framed pictures to the floor as I tried valiantly to escape.

When my legs gave out altogether, I commando crawled, my entire body starting to go numb. I looked toward the door, only a few short feet away, but it may as well have been miles as my body succumbed to whatever it was she'd dosed me with.

A shadow appeared in front of me. A small shadow. I lifted my head again, its weight getting heavier by the second, and spied Thor through the glass panel in the bottom of the door.

"Human?" He cocked his head and looked at me.

I reached out a hand toward him. "Help," I croaked before my arm dropped, followed by my head. My forehead met the floor with a thunk. I don't know if Thor heard me, or understood, and I no longer had control of the muscles in my neck, which meant I couldn't turn it and my nose was now squashed into the floor, making breathing incredibly difficult. The only silver lining was that it didn't hurt. I was numb. My entire body was numb. And paralyzed. Except I was breathing, albeit with difficulty through my squashed nose. I lay in the hall and listened as Mrs. Hill moved about, clearing up our afternoon tea, I assumed. Then her footsteps were coming my way and I was flipped onto my back.

"All numb, dear?" she asked conversationally. I blinked. Oh good. My eyelids still worked. And my lungs. Although neither of those things was going to help me get out of here and away from Mrs. Crazy Pants. Seemed Brett Baxter wasn't the only nut job in the family.

She leaned down and grabbed my ankle, her grip surprisingly strong. I was even more surprised when she began to drag me down the hallway. This woman was seventy years old. How could she possibly drag a one hundred and thirty-pound dead weight?

"If people would just learn to mind their own business," she said as she dragged me along the floor, "then this sort of thing wouldn't happen."

I blame the fact that I was drugged that it took me so long to figure it out. Of course, now that we were here, with her dragging me along totally helpless, things finally fell into place. Mrs. Hill had killed Ben. I didn't know why, yet, but it was linked to Brett. That's when she'd decided to take me out too. When I asked about her nephew. Clearly it had been a surprise to her, but she'd rallied quickly, hatched up a plan to get me into her house and ingesting poison. And it worked. I'd fallen for it hook, line and sinker.

My head ricocheted off a doorframe as she dragged me into a room near the front of the house.

"Sorry about that, dear," she apologized. I lay staring at the ceiling. It had stickers on it. They were faint, but I could just make out they were stars. She dropped my leg and left me in the center of the room. I heard the sound of curtains screeching across the rails and the room was plunged into semi-darkness. The stars on the ceiling began to glow and I blinked. Cool. I tried to remember my astronomy classes from school, wondered if the stars were a certain constellation but came up blank.

I could hear Mrs. Hill moving about to my left, then she was back, and with her foot, she turned my head until I could see whatever it was she wanted me to see. And then it all became crystal clear. There, in my line of vision, was an altar. Actually it was probably a dresser, but it was draped in a black cloth and it had candles on it, and a chalice and some other stuff I couldn't actually see from my vantage point on the floor. But what sealed the deal was what I was lying on. Etched into the floor was a pentagram—well, half of one, since I was lying right on top of it. Holy heck, Brett Baxter had been right about the witches. Had he suspected his aunt? But he hadn't mentioned her specifically when I asked him about his case, and Ben had made no mention of it in his notes. But to be fair, Ben hadn't taken any notes on Brett's case at all.

I was feeling strangely calm as I lay there and put all the pieces together. Somehow Mrs. Hill must have got wind that Ben was looking into the whole witchcraft thing and killed him before he could out her. Which was a tad extreme. I also noticed something else. The numbness pervading my body was fading and I was getting a pins and needles sensation in my fingers and face. I couldn't have gotten the full dose since I hadn't drunk all of the tea. I could only hope Mrs. Hill failed to take that into the equation.

She was flicking through a book, licking her finger and pinching the corner of each page, scanning the contents, only to lick and flick again. Eventually, she settled on a page. "Yes. That should do it," she murmured before she picked up a knife. A big, sharp-looking knife that looked strangely familiar. Was it Ben's? Of course, lying here solving the mystery of Ben's murder was one thing, but seeing that knife in her hand, the way the candlelight glinted off the blade, drove it home to me. She intended to kill me, right here, right now. I had to do something. I couldn't lie here and accept my fate so meekly. Easy enough to say if I weren't partially paralyzed. I willed the drug to leave my system faster, experimented with moving my fingers, seeing how much movement had returned, all without tipping her off. Get her talking. Distract her.

I made a garbled noise in my throat and she

glanced at me, almost surprised to find me on her floor. "Oh, I suppose you're wondering what's going on, Audrey dear?" She sounded positively friendly.

"You see, my silly nosy nephew was poking his nose in where it doesn't belong and stumbled upon this." She indicated the room we were now in. "So of course he wanted to know all about it, and wanted to join my coven. I couldn't have that. The truth is, I'm just a dabbler. I needed a hobby to keep me occupied during the winter months when the garden is dormant. And I actually got the idea from Brett himself." She laughed. "He was spouting on about his theories one Sunday at lunch and he landed on magic and witchcraft and I admit, it piqued my interest. I mean it's mostly herbs and crystals and meditation, you know? But I created a wonderful tonic for my garden. Have you seen my hyacinths this season?"

I hmmd in my throat. Keep talking, Crazy Pants. "The last thing I needed was Brett telling everyone. I mean, really? Witchcraft?" She tsked. "Then the stupid boy goes and hires my neighbor to investigate! Can you believe it? He thought I was lying about not having a coven and that brain of his, well, it just doesn't fire on all cylinders I'm afraid. So of course every woman he crossed paths with was a potential witch and he just had to know. You know?"

I knew they were both bat shit crazy. Instead, I blinked and made another murmuring noise in my throat.

"I didn't mean to kill Ben." She was examining the knife now. "I popped over to make sure he understood that what Brett had hired him for was pure nonsense. He was in the kitchen, cleaning up— such a house proud young man—and he was hand washing some cutlery he didn't want to put in the dishwasher, so I picked up the tea towel and began drying. I didn't think anything of it. And then..." She paused and I gurgled for her to continue. "I got a little agitated. He's sharp. Put two and two together straightaway and asked me outright if I was practicing witchcraft. And he kinda turned toward me and I was just so shocked I shoved this into his belly." She indicated the blade in her hand. "I don't know who was more surprised!" Her voice went up and she clutched at her pearls. "Me or Ben. I mean, I was aghast and I pulled the knife out and he's clutching his stomach and blood is coming out and he looks at me with this stunned expression on his face." She was silent for a moment, remembering. "But then I had a thought. I could fix him. There had to be a spell that would heal him. But he was losing a lot of blood and then I remembered I'd watched something on one of those hospital shows on television that you shouldn't take the knife out? When you have an injury with a foreign body, you should leave the object in as it could be stopping the blood flow. So I put the knife back."

I blinked. Twice. That would explain the two stab wounds. "Only that didn't go so well and blood started coming out of his mouth. I thought if I could get him to my clearing in the woods where I practice moon magic, he'd be okay, the moon would help heal him while I ran back to get my spell book. I helped him outside, he was fine, doing well actually, and we got across the lawn and then he just went down like a ton of bricks. I had to drag him the rest of the way. But we got there, and I lit the candle I keep hidden in some undergrowth and made sure a ray of moonlight was touching him and then I came back here to get my spell book." She twisted her pearls. "I don't know what went wrong." Her voice had dropped to a whisper. "Maybe I took too long? It did take me awhile to find a healing spell for such an injury. Most are spells for illnesses, not for..." She drifted off, then blinked and visibly shook. "When I went back to the clearing...he was dead."

I wanted to rant at her. I wanted to rave. Why didn't she just call him an ambulance? Why didn't she try and stop the bleeding with the tea towel and not shove the knife back into him? She could have saved him! My eyes filled with tears and I blinked hard to dispel them. It was pointless. His death was pointless.

Mrs. Hill pulled herself together and narrowed her eyes at me. "Anyway," she said with a sniff, "what's done is done and it cannot be undone."

You got that right, lady. My eyes darted around the room looking for something, anything, that I could use as a weapon. Slim pickings. The numbness was slowly leaving my body, and in its wake, the worst case of pins and needles known to mankind. I wanted to twitch and rub at my skin so badly but didn't want to give away the fact I could move. Well, parts of me could, pretty sure my legs were still numb. Then Mrs. Hill began some sort of chant about earth, wind, and fire. I wasn't paying too much attention until she was standing over me, straddling me with a foot either side of my hips. She could move fast for a senior citizen. What had me really concerned though was the carving knife clutched in her hands and the crazed expression on her face. She was going to do this, she was going to plunge that knife into my chest. I vaguely wondered what the rest of her plan was. Chop me up and use me as compost in her garden? Actually that wouldn't be a bad way to get rid of a body, I supposed.

Thankfully Mrs. Hill had one weakness. Arthritic knees. It took her a bit to lower herself so she was sitting on my abdomen, and when she did, it was her full weight. I made a small woof as she squashed the air out of me. I'm not sure, I may have peed a little too, with her weight right on my bladder and my body still battling the numbing agent she'd slipped me it was hard to say.

Her chanting continued, something about the moon goddess—I wasn't sure if whatever spell she was trying to cast was kosher since we were actually indoors beneath a ceiling of fake stars and not a moon in sight. She held the knife in both hands above her head, then it was swinging down, aiming for my heart. My hands shot up and grabbed her wrists, holding her off. Her face registered her surprise. Oh yeah, Crazy Pants, weren't expecting that, were you? Ordinarily, it wouldn't have been a fair fight. I'm young, fit, healthy and strong. She's an old lady with arthritis—although it didn't seem to slow her down much and I wondered if she was using her magical herbs to help with that.

Regardless, currently, I wasn't in top form having been poisoned by the crazy one, so we were at a Mexican standoff, with her perched on top of me and the knife between us. My arms were trembling and the pins and needles had my teeth on edge, stinging my nerve endings until I wanted to scream. Sweat beaded on my forehead. If I could manage a hip thrust I could probably buck her off me, but my lower body was still suffering the effects of her poison and all I could manage was a pathetic leg flop, which did exactly nothing.

We were both grunting and the knife was making slow progress toward my chest when there was a crash and booted feet thundered into the hallway. I almost sagged in relief, only that would have been a mistake—then the knife would have found its target. Wouldn't that be ironic? Distracted by the cavalry and end up dying just as I'm being rescued!

"Drop the weapon! Hands on your head!" Galloway shouted from the doorway. Out the corner of my eye, I saw him there, feet planted, gun drawn and aimed at Mrs. Hill's chest. He'd never looked so goddamn sexy. My heart did a little flutter.

Mrs. Hill released the knife, which of course fell straight toward me. Releasing her wrists, my fingers managed to wrap around the blade before the tip embedded itself in my heart, although it was doubtful it would have met its target without her thrusting it into me. My arms dropped to my side, the knife slipped out of my grasp and skidded a few inches away.

Galloway holstered his weapon and approached, cuffing Mrs. Hill before lifting her off me. I closed my eyes in relief, and also said a little prayer that I hadn't peed. That would be mortifying with Captain Cowboy Hot Pants standing over me.

"You okay?" he glanced down at me.

"Sure." I grinned. It was a total lie of course. My entire body was zinging and zapping like I'd been electrified, but I put on a brave face. "How did you know I was here?"

"Weirdest thing. I got a call from your number, but all I could hear was a cat meowing. I thought you'd butt-dialed me so I hung up. Only it rang again and it was the same thing. Now, I don't speak cat, but this one was really insistent so I figured I'd drop by and check in on you, make sure everything was okay."

Thor, bless his heart, had called for help. I was going to buy that cat a lobster dinner. Galloway continued, "Your garage was open, but there was no sign of you. Then the cat streaked past me and over to here, scratching at the front door. I took a calculated risk that you were inside and in trouble."

"Good guess." I nodded.

"Gut instinct." He had Mrs. Hill pushed face-first against the wall. His eyes ran over me, lingered on my hand, before moving to my face. I glanced at my hand too, saw the blood, realized I'd sliced my fingers open when I'd grabbed the blade when Mrs. Hill had dropped it.

"It's fine," I told him. "Just a nick."

"Can you get up?"

"Ummm. Possibly?" Although my legs were on fire with pins and needles I wasn't positive they could hold my weight yet. I nodded toward Mrs. Hill, who, for once in her life, was mercifully silent. "She poisoned me. Something in the tea. I couldn't move at all initially, some sort of paralysis, but now it's wearing off and I've got the worst case of pins and needles. Stings like a bitch."

Galloway tugged on the cuffs holding Mrs. Hills's wrists behind her back. "What did you give her?"

"Relax. It was just Crimson Bark. Like she said, it's wearing off. The effects are only temporary." She shot me a look I couldn't read. I swear she had a gleam in her eye. Was there something else in the tea she wasn't telling me about?

23

I heard the sound of approaching sirens, screeching tires and car doors slamming, then the place exploded with activity. Galloway handed Mrs. Hill over to Officer Jacobs, watched and listened as Jacobs read her rights, then led her away. Sergeant Young accompanied her, then Sergeant Clements and Officer Mills turned up and I bit my lip to keep from groaning out loud.

"Are the medics here yet?" Galloway asked.

"Just pulling up." Clements nodded, standing in the doorway with his thumbs hooked in his belt loops, eyeballing me where I still lay on the floor.

"Gloves on," Galloway told them. "I want everything in this room photographed, bagged, and taken in."

Mills snorted. "That's a lot of work, Detective. Surely you just need the knife?" He nodded toward the knife by my side.

"Everything. I'll be checking. Make sure you're thorough," Galloway ground out. "I'll make it easier for you though, since it's oh so hard." His sarcasm was unmistakable and I wanted to clap my hands in approval. Opening the forensics case Sergeant Young had brought in, Galloway snapped on a glove and shook out a plastic evidence bag. Then he stepped over me with a gruff apology and bagged the knife. He handed it to Young. "Take this back to the station with you. I want it expedited. Find out if it was the murder weapon used to kill Benjamin Delaney."

"On it." She nodded, accepting the bag. "We're taking Hill in now. Or did you want us to hang around longer, assist with the scene?"

Galloway inclined his head. "You can go."

Two EMTs appeared in the doorway. "This our patient?"

Pretty good guess since I was the only one on the floor, but again, I kept my observations to myself.

"We can't let you in there," Mills told them. "It's a crime scene."

Galloway rolled his eyes, but before he could say

anything one of the EMTs eyeballed Mills and snapped, "She's our patient. She trumps any crime scene." And pushed past him, coming to kneel by my side. I could have kissed him.

"How you feeling, ma'am?" he asked. He whipped out a blood pressure cuff and began taking my vitals. He was nice, mid-forties, with a friendly smile and take no shit attitude. I decided we should be friends.

"Mrs. Crazy Pants poisoned me," I told him, "With something called Crimson Bark. Heard of it?"

The younger EMT snorted. "Mrs. Crazy Pants. I like it." This one looked about twelve, but I figured he had to be in his twenties somewhere. "I'm Ned, this is Jayce," he said.

"Audrey." I smiled, taking a liking to the two paramedics.

"Take a look at that hand will you, Ned?" Jayce instructed. Putting his stethoscope in his ears he held up the other end and said, "I'm just going to listen to your heart, okay?"

"Sure." I lay there while Jayce moved the stethoscope around my chest and Ned prodded at my hand. "I think we can get away with dressing these. The cuts aren't deep so we won't need sutures," he commented.

I wasn't sure if he was talking to me or Jayce, but

I answered anyway. "Suits me. Just patch me up. I don't want to go to the hospital."

"You probably should. Just to get checked out by a doctor," he replied, bandaging my hand.

Jayce finished listening to my internal organs and put the stethoscope away. "All good." He grinned. "So tell me about this poison. What were the symptoms?"

I told him what happened, how my body had gone completely numb but now I almost had full feeling back and even the pins and needles were starting to abate. Jayce nodded. "Fast-acting but leaves the system quickly too. Ned is right, you should get checked out at the hospital just to be sure whatever you ingested doesn't have any lasting effects on your liver or kidneys."

"Do I have to go in the ambulance?"

"Not if you don't want to. I think you're okay to come in under your own steam. Just make sure you get checked out, okay?" They helped me to my feet, made sure I was steady and that the feeling had returned to my legs. Ned had been doing something on his phone when he glanced at me, face unsure. "Errrr," he said.

"What?"

"You said Crimson Bark, right? That the old lady

laced your drink with?"

I nodded. "That's right. Why? Is Jayce right, has it eaten away my liver and I don't even know it yet?" Panic laced my words.

He chuckled, "No, no. Reading this, it does no lasting damage. But..." He held out the screen for me to read.

"Oh." I gulped.

"What?" Galloway demanded. He'd been so silent, watching proceedings this entire time that I'd actually forgotten he was there. "What does it say? What's wrong?"

I was shaking my head and snapped a warning glance at Ned who held up his hands. "Nothing. It's not important," I told Galloway.

"Gentlemen?" Galloway addressed Jayce and Ned who both shrugged their shoulders, picked up their bags and saluted farewell to me. "Take care, Audrey. Try and stay away from crazy pants old ladies, huh?"

"No promises." I grinned, giving them a wave, then I turned my attention to Galloway. "Okay, I know you're going to want me to come into the station and give a statement, and you're going to want a DNA sample because it's my blood on the knife, and my fingerprints and all of that stuff," I began, "but can I just pop home for a minute first? I could really use the bathroom and to freshen up."

He frowned. "Everything okay?"

"Yup." I nodded. Then I felt it. The first gurgling's. Placing my hand over my belly I smiled sweetly. "All good." I had to get home. Fast. Pushing past Galloway I called out over my shoulder, "I'm fine, I promise. I'll just freshen up and then come down to the station. I'll see you there." With a wave, I was gone. Out the front door that hung off its hinges, across the lawn, up Ben's driveway where Ben and Thor were waiting for me.

"God, Audrey, are you okay? You're hurt! What happened?" Ben floated along beside me as I made a beeline for the front door. My focus entirely on getting myself to the sanctuary of Ben's house before the storm that was about to come was unleashed.

"Audrey?" Ben pressed when I didn't answer him. Truth was, I couldn't. I was wildly recalculating my options, for the rolling in my abdomen was clear. Armageddon was coming, I was out of time. Moving as fast as my clenched ass would take me, I made it inside and into the bathroom, slamming the door in Ben's face. Which made zero difference because he simply floated right on through. Fingers frantically undoing my jeans, I totally ignored him, which should have been an indication to him that shit was about to go down. To give him credit, when I started doing a mad bunny hop and pulling my jeans down at the same time, he did squeak "oh" and hurried out of the bathroom. From the other side of the door, he called, "Fitz? You okay in there?"

I made it to the toilet with seconds to spare and there I spent the worst twenty minutes of my life. Oh. My. God. The noises. The smell. The burning! When the storm had passed I sat there, gathering myself. One thing I'd learned about Crimson Bark— its effects were fast. Fast to hit and fast to leave. But just in case, I remained seated and told Ben what had happened through the door.

"Do you think that's why I couldn't get into her house?" he asked. "She used some sort of spell to keep me out?"

I recalled Ben had said he couldn't enter Mrs. Hill's place, but I hadn't paid it any attention. "She doesn't know you're a ghost though. Well, at least I don't think she does. She never mentioned it, and at the end there, well, she wasn't hiding anything."

"So maybe some sort of ward or sigil or something that protects her house from spirits?"

"You could be onto something. There's a sigil burned into the wood on the gate between your place and hers. I've never thought anything of it until now. Enough about me, what about you?" I yelled at the door.

"What about me?" He sounded puzzled.

"You phoned Galloway! How did you do that?"

"Ahhh. It wasn't me. Not exactly. I instructed Thor on what to do. He dragged your phone out of your bag, held his paw on the last dialed number and told Kade that you needed help. Of course, Kade didn't understand any of it and hung up. So we rang back."

"Genius," I muttered. With no action for at least ten minutes, I figured I was safe, and weakly peeled myself off the toilet, kicked my jeans off because I didn't think I could stand the pressure of denim against my butt, and washed my hands. Well, one hand, since the other was out of commission thanks to Mrs. Crazy Pants. Dressed in T-shirt and panties I opened the door, gasping in the sweet fresh air. "I think the bathroom is going to need a fresh coat of paint."

"Everything okay?" Galloway drawled.

"Argh!" Shit. Poo. Bum. How long had he been standing there? Did he hear... I closed my eyes, not wanting to think about what had just transpired in the bathroom. Then another thought. Did he hear me talking to Ben? About ghosts? But I figured Ben would have warned me if that were the case. Wouldn't he? The dirty rat had disappeared, leaving me dressed in my underwear to face Captain Cowboy Hot Pants alone.

"Audrey Fitzgerald," Galloway said, grinning, dimple flashing, "working with you is going to be interesting, to say the least."

Oh sugar, you don't know the half of it.

Book two, **Give up the Ghost** is available here: http://mybook.to/GUTG

Thank you for reading, if you enjoyed **Ghost Mortem**, please consider leaving a review.

If you'd like to find a complete list of my books, including series and reading order, please visit my website at:

https://janehinchey.com

Also, if you'd like to sign up to receive emails with the latest news, exclusive offers and more, you can do that here:

Janehinchey.com/join-my-newsletter

And finally, if social media is your jam, you're

welcome to join my readers group, Little Devils, on Facebook here:

**https://www.facebook.com/
groups/JanesLittleDevils/**

Thank you so much for taking a chance and reading my book - I do this for you.

xoxo

Jane

FREE BOOK OFFER

Want to get an email alert when the next Ghost
Detective Mystery is available?

Sign up for my Reader's Group today,

https://janehinchey.com/newsletter-giveaway-
signup/

and as a bonus, receive a FREE e-book of **Cupcakes
& Curses!**

Want to read more cozy mysteries with magic and mayhem? Of course you do!

Books in the Witch Way Series:

#1 Witch Way to Murder & Mayhem

#2 Witch Way to Romance & Ruin

#3 Witch Way Down Under

#4 Witch Way to Beauty and the Beach

#5 Witch Way to Death & Destruction

FOR A FULL LIST OF JANE HINCHEY BOOKS VISIT
www.JaneHinchey.com/books

ABOUT JANE

 Aussie Author & International Bestseller Jane Hinchey writes sexy, snarky, badass, urban fantasies and funny, witchy, paranormal cozy mysteries.

Living in the City of Churches (aka Adelaide, South Australia) with her man, two cats, and turtle, she would really prefer to live in a magical town where cooking could be done with a snap of her fingers, and her house would clean itself.

When she's not in her writing cave she's usually playing the Sims, Civilizations or something similar, binge-watching Netflix or upping the ante in the crazy cat lady stakes.

Explore Jane's worlds, get writing tips, and join her newsletter at https://janehinchey.com/join-my-newsletter/ for book news, book sales and laughter! If emails aren't your thing, then join her Facebook Reader Group - Jane's Little Devils!

If you liked this book, please take a few minutes

to leave a review for it. Authors (Jane included) really appreciate this, and it helps draw more readers to books they might like. Thanks!

facebook.com/janehincheyauthor
twitter.com/janehinchey
instagram.com/janehincheyauthor

CPSIA information can be obtained
at www.ICGtesting.com
Printed in the USA
BVHW040228020522
635878BV00011B/39